A Castle in Romagna

A Castle in Romagna

by Igor Štiks

translated from the Croatian by Tomislav Kuzmanović
and Russell Scott Valentino

AB
Autumn Hill Books
Iowa City, Iowa

ÆB

Autumn Hill Books, Iowa City 52240
© 2004 by Autumn Hill Books
All Rights Reserved. Published 2004
Printed in the United States of America

Originally published as *Dvorac u Romagni*
© 2000 by Durieux, Zagreb, Croatia

Autumn Hill ISBN 0-9754444-0-9

Book Design and Layout by Nicole Flores

for M.

As one comes down the old road from Rimini, near Cesena, the forest oaks form a pleasant, secure umbrella against the scorching heat. After some ten meandering kilometers, at the top of a hill that the road cuts through, one catches a glimpse of the Castello Mardi. Its roofs shine in the afternoon sun, and it seems as though it has fused at a slant with the gentle surroundings.

Come nearer and it offers the chance to examine renowned frescoes and study all the beauty of early Renaissance architectural skill. One may also descend the two hundred thirteen steps that lead to the dungeon in which Enzo Strecci, that giant of Renaissance literature, spent days of hardship awaiting his death. He was the main reason I decided to visit Mardi Castle.

There were three of us, two girls and I, on a beautiful summer day, which was reflected in the red faces of the breathless friar-caretakers of the castle and its garden. They directed us — "*a destra, a destra*" — toward the tourist portion of the edifice. All the way to where the friar sold the tickets and offered select information about the history of the castle, we could feel a slight draft and smell the damp coming through the dungeon bars at the bottom of the wall. Here and there we could see a sword or mace or hear a voice from the cellar, as if Strecci himself were still protesting his innocence.

The first thing I noticed about the friar, with whom it turned out I was to stay until evening, was his unruly hair and luxuriant curls, hanging like bunches of grapes all about his round face. He waited for us, the tickets in his outstretched hands and a prepared smile of warm welcome on his face. There followed a lecture on the most interesting curiosities of the castle and then—because, as he put it, one has to make a living—he requested five thousand lire for the free tour. While he was putting the money into a box, probably in order to break the awkward silence that had followed his last words, he asked kindly, "*Da dove venite, ragazze?* (Where are you girls from?)"

Marianna said, "*La Francia*," Irena said the same, and he turned to me and asked, "*E tu, bambino?* (And you, child?)"

"*Sono bosniaco* (I'm a Bosnian)," I said reservedly, which made the friar suddenly break into loud laughter and blurt out, looking me straight in the eye, "Bang, bang. Eh? Eh? *Bosniaco.* Bang, bang."

I stood before him, utterly bewildered, unable to think of any words in Italian that might serve as a response. "*Capisci?* Bang, bang," he said again, this time without gesturing in my face, waiting for a reaction to his all too obvious joke: it was the summer of 1995.

"We should get going," said the girls, who were ready for the tour.

"Man this guy's nuts," I told them, looking at the stiff grimace on his face, upon which he answered with yet another surprise, uttered in Croatian: "Maybe nuts but safe at least, eh? What do you say to that, Bosnian?"

"I'd better listen to the girls," I said. Suddenly he grabbed my hand and changed his tone. Once again he was the pleasant friar selling tickets, maybe even more pleasant because of the language only the two of us in the room and, it would seem, the general vicinity, shared.

"Just a joke, eh? *Capisci?* No harm intended. It's been a long time since I saw anybody from home. At least up close."

That was the first time I wondered how old he might be. Only after he had mentioned time and suggested proof of his age, putting his hand on mine long enough for its surface to remind me of a layer of cream cut through with barely visible veins, only then did I look at him more carefully. Later I understood that he was over sixty-five.

There was a brief moment of silence, and you could hear the girls in the next room, admiring the accomplishments of Renaissance wall painting.

"I'm an exile, an '*esulo*,' like you a little," he went on, without letting me interrupt.

I tried to explain that I was in a hurry. He let go of my hand and said, "I wouldn't want you to be angry. It was just a joke. You're not mad, are you? It must make you happy that I speak so well. Before you is living proof that the language of one's early days is not easily forgotten. That feeling doesn't grow old, you know. Yes, yes, no more terra nostra. Good-bye. Never again, *mai più*, back home. Bang, bang, like I said. See you when we free you, as they used to put it. Isn't that right? Or am I making things up?"

He didn't wait for my answer.

"I haven't run into anyone from there for a long time, a really long time. Forgive me. Have a cigarette. I wouldn't want to part with yet another Slav this way. You're not angry? Are we okay?"

In the hope of getting rid of him for good, I said it hadn't even crossed my mind, I was just a little unpleasantly surprised, I didn't want to talk about it, I was on vacation, I was in the company of two angels who didn't like to wait and, besides, I had paid for the ticket, so it wouldn't be right for me not to see where the renowned Enzo Strecci had spent his last days.

At this the friar gave a knowing grin. "Enzo Strecci, yes. Yes. Enzo the Great. You won't believe it if I tell you that he was like you and me. No, you won't believe it. Just like you and me."

He uttered every syllable of the last phrase as if it were part of a plot, opening his eyes wide to emphasize our newfound closeness.

"Really?" I said with some interest.

He immediately went on, "Yes, really. I sometimes think that that's the only reason I'm still here. As if all my life I've been executing other people's wills. Others know better than I that that is not an easy thing to do. 'Let what has come upon me be remembered,' as Enzo says somewhere in his book of poetry, if I remember correctly."

I nodded. It was clear that we could share an interest in Strecci if the connection between us rested on a firmer foundation. As I write about it today, I think it was just then that I tried for the last time to remedy the tiny misstep on our intended journey into the Renaissance. But I didn't get far. It's a point of personal consolation to me that I stayed with the friar that whole afternoon. And, in the end, that is what made this story possible.

I had taken a few steps in the direction that the girls had

disappeared when he called me back and, his face to the window, began to speak. I looked at his bent round back, and that was how it began, when he stretched out his hand and said, "Come here. Look. That way there, up the hill, that's the path on which Enzo Strecci, the handsome Lombardian, came to this place. Come. Take a look at that path."

I couldn't leave him after that.

Chapter the First

It is said that he appeared on that road early one autumn morning, several months after the Habsburgs had taken Lombardy. It was the year 1535. The influential merchant Strecci had sent his son to his wife's homeland, which is how Enzo ended up approaching the castle that morning, carrying a letter for Francesco Mardi. In it his good friend Federico Strecci asked that, during those confusing times, which needed no lengthy description, he might look after Enzo, who he believed, so the letter stated, could put his poetic skills to better use in this new environment by shortening the rainy afternoons and assuaging the boredom of Mardi's ladies than by disturbing the master's peace, an activity at which, it seemed, the young man had shown aptitude these last months.

And so, when the twenty-five year old youth stepped toward the brass doors of Mardi Castle, he had a smile on his face that neither the guards nor the long wait before the master's door could wipe clean. For it was the kind of smile that gave one the false impression that the future into which one was headed, oblivious of potential danger, could erase the memory of recent peril. And he did not have to wait long to confirm his impression, to see that the feeling did not lie, and that good fortune had at last caressed his brown hair. Just before noon she passed through the chamber where he awaited his reception.

Now then, if you know the story of Strecci's fate, you won't find it difficult to recognize the beautiful Catarina in it, Mardi's young wife, who at that moment strode by, accompanied by her dear friend and chambermaid Maria. We can only imagine—though something about it is reported by the investigator into the future mess, the bishop's examiner Fra Giovanni, who for several hours questioned the chambermaid in connection with this unpleasant affair—that Enzo quickly got to his feet, that Catarina passed without even noticing him, that he watched her walk until the moment when that little serpent Maria stopped before his handsome face to make her presence known.

"Does the gentleman have no eyes?" said the sweet lamb.

At which Enzo turned and, confused by the sight before him, blurted out the honest, reckless words, "Forgive me, Miss. I hadn't even seen you."

She quickly followed her mistress without replying, and Enzo collapsed onto a bench and fell into a fateful reverie.

There you have it. That was the whole thing, you could say—nothing special, an opportunity, a few words preached to the winds, so to speak; but like it or not, that's the way the affair began: the seed of love, whether you believe in it or not, had taken root in the hearts of the two young people, while the third did not even suspect, and the fourth was preparing to do a good deed. And while you're still thinking that your fate is written in the stars, forget it, brother. Someone has already begun spinning the thread to fool you, so it usually happens, through a favorable horoscope prediction.

Soon after, the white-haired Mardi welcomed the youth and generously offered him chambers in the right wing of the castle, ordered that water should be heated for the traveler, and wished him pleasurable days of repose following all the troubles from which he had luckily escaped through his flight, for which Mardi had a remedy, or at least so it seemed when, tapping his shoulder to the rhythm of his words, he said, "I respect your father too much to deprive you of anything, my son. I believe you will find comfort and happiness in your mother's homeland. During your stay, I will be happy to share all that I have with you, dear Enzo."

Strecci thanked him politely for this expression of sincere sympathy, and thought, still under the impression of his meeting with Catarina, that he had to admit there really was something to what the old man had said. Tempting fate, for he was a young man and, besides, he was convinced that God himself would forgive a good joke, he wondered excitedly whether there was anything more natural than the fact that we love what our friends love, and then, unselfishly why not, he added this to Mardi's offer: If God is willing, and the hero's luck holds, then she too, my dear Mardi, will be shared between us.

2

At this point, where the story of Enzo Strecci begins for the reader, allow me to skip a few hours and alter the sequence of events of that afternoon for my story, skipping to the moment when the sun was barely visible from the window of the friar's chamber, in order to make my account more successful, so that I might begin a second story and weave it into the first, for they are inextricably linked in my memory and, in any case, it's perhaps the best kind of story telling of all.

I leaned back in my chair after a few sentences, having forgotten my initial anger and why and with whom I had come here. During the entire length of the story of Enzo Strecci's fate, the friar would stand up, act out scenes, make speeches, imitate characters, express their thoughts and dreams, and convey the contents of letters and official documents. He was truly an omniscient narrator, a fact evident from the first part of this story.

"Now that's practically literature!" I cried when he had finished the story of Enzo. "It's clear you know a lot about him."

"As I told you, young man," answered the friar, "sometimes it seems to me it's the only reason I'm here. Somehow, regardless of time and space, Strecci and I are connected. Someone once said that we listen to stories and read books only to know we're not alone. I would add that the fact that we collect them, listen to them, or read them persistently all our lives, speaks of our desire to surpass their uniqueness. Somewhere stories come together, perhaps crossing or overlapping, but they are never the same. Neither life nor literature, my boy, is heraldic. You know, on one coat of arms, in the upper right corner, the same coat of arms is repeated. And in its upper right corner, it's repeated again, just smaller this time, and so on to infinity. That's never successful. The only thing that remains is the interweaving, the coming together of fates. I believe that every story has a relative, even if it's reversed, which of course one must recognize."

The friar nodded as if to emphasize his words.

"Besides knowing the fate of Enzo Strecci, you know Croatian quite well," I said in praise, still under the impression of what he had told me.

"I'm from the island of Rab after all!" he exclaimed. "As far as I know, they speak Croatian well there," he said, laughing at his own joke.

"When did you leave? Why?"

"The summer of forty-eight, nearly fifty years ago. It was a rough time is why."

"Isn't that around the time of the Information Bureau's resolution, Tito's break with Stalin?" I asked, making my interest clear to him.

"That's just it, young man." The friar stood up from his chair and walked to the window.

"Was that the reason?" I asked in anticipation, not realizing that my question would begin a new story, this time his own, in which variations were not allowed and humor would find little place.

Outside, the woods had enveloped the sun, but the sultriness did not disappear with it. The friar turned, came back to his chair, sighed, and began speaking as one speaks about something precious, slowly, choosing his words with care, in the hope of being completely understood. The sky darkened still further, becoming in the end a mantle of shining stars, and his story unfolded.

"It's one of the reasons," he said. "It was unspeakably hot the summer of forty-eight, a bit like this one. I was returning by boat from Trieste a few days following the Resolution. You couldn't say where it was worse, above deck, wetting your head every once in a while, or below, where you couldn't breath. As you know, it was issued at the beginning of July. I was coming back from Trieste, as I said, where I'd gone a couple of days before with the intention of staying in Italy. My father had persuaded me to go, and for two or three days I had tried to obtain the necessary documents from the refugee office. I have to say that on Rab that unspeakably hot forty-eight, only a few Italian families were left, and it was clear, as things were going in those days, that soon there would be even fewer. My father liked to pride himself on his solidarity among them, claiming that there was no force that could expel him from the land he had fought for. Until recently unassuming, and—with our family at least—unified, the neighbors threw rocks in our windows, avoided handshakes and greetings, and even sometimes shouted insults after us. But that year we had already accepted such things as an inefficient and benign means of intimidation and pressure to leave. After father's expulsion from the party in May of 1946, which was based on his having helped some relatives who turned out to have several fascists in their family, the security police became regular guests in our house. My father was hard hit by the betrayal of his comrades, with whom he had until just the day before shared the adversities of the war and the post-war year, putting the country, as they used to say, on a new foundation. He tried in vain to justify himself before the authorities, asking to be rehabilitated, until the very day they found him lying helpless on the veranda, his heart giving out.

"Just as I was approaching Rab by boat, he lay almost motionless, imprisoned in the Benedictine Monastery, maybe just a bit more at peace in the false conviction that I at least was safe. Here then. This is how it all happened.

"The heart attack destroyed him. Afterward he was taken care of by old Ivanka, long since a member of our family, a woman who'd been my second mother and nanny. My mother had been cut down by pneumonia back in 1940.

"After his expulsion from the Party, my father was saved from harsher punishment by his firm commitment to communism and his considerable contribution, as it used to be said, to the battle in our region. Or I'm mistaken, for maybe the leniency of the authorities, which consisted in subjecting him to isolation, was caused simply by the fact that someone in the right place — and in those times such was the rule — put in a good word for him, in the same way that some falsehood or other had been attributed to him before.

"Because of my father's convictions and quick decision to join the national struggle, I spent my early days hiding in the homes of Partisans on our island. And that's the answer to your question about why I speak Croatian so well to this day.

"The end of the war changed our situation only for a short time. The difference turned on the fact that before we had hidden in other people's homes while now we hid in our own.

"After the heart attack my father was seized by a fearful panic for my future. The news of the clash with Russia only added to it. From the day he was confined to his bed, he often spoke angrily, as much as he was able, about how there was no longer any life for us there, and how they were going to look for scapegoats among us (he meant the Italians). Afterward, he'd say, the meek would single themselves out. Then he would add bitterly that things had turned into a mess, that the story had come to an end, and world communism would have to find some other place to show its feasibility. Still, even until the night when we heard about the Resolution, he had never definitively set the day for my departure. Today I think that my presence dispersed the gloomy thoughts that come to the mind of a man in such a position and hasten the final hour. I comforted him as much as I could, along with old Ivanka, and closed the blinds and pulled the curtains shut. I tried hard to prevent anything from disturbing him and secretly prayed in the kitchen for his salvation.

"I could not let him see, in his condition, that reactionary forces flourished in his very own house.

"Why didn't I listen to him and prepare the documents in Trieste? Why didn't I listen to my dying father? Did I think I could survive? How could it be that the departure of my family and friends did not suggest to me that I should follow their example? Why did I want to remain in a town that was becoming less and less mine, in which there were fewer people every day who were glad to see me? I assume that these are the questions running through your mind.

"They all have just one answer. But let's do things in order. Let's present them in their true light, without forgetting the details. Let's expose the traps of fate."

Chapter the Second

Even if the devil himself had prepared her for that altogether unexceptional dinner, her appearance at the moment she entered the Mardi dining hall would not have caused Enzo to renounce all the caution and moral scruples that had periodically tormented his conscience while he relaxed in his warm bath. Then again, if he had not had such a captivating smile and promising build, perhaps the lady of the house would not have dared disturb her peaceful idleness.

"So you're the gentleman from Lombardy," she said briefly and coquettishly. "I am honored you're to be our guest. Now that I've taken a closer look, I completely understand my maid's flush."

Gazing upon the apparition that had uttered these words, Enzo shivered, but then more soberly and with a slight sense of resentment, thought: Does she take me for a child? What maid, dammit? It's my custom to first address the master upon entering another's house. That motto, which made him laugh good-heartedly at himself, brought the blood back into his face.

Raising an eyebrow, he dared to toss out his first bait: "Where the maidservants are in competition with their mistresses, the people must be truly marvelous."

It seemed to Catarina in the first instant that the youngster was rather crude, but also, to an equal if not greater extent, sweet. After several moments of indecision, her initial attraction gained the upper hand. Mardi laughed aloud and added, as if God himself were his prod, "It would already seem, dear Enzo, that in this country you will find a wife, too."

In pronouncing these words, Mardi confirmed that it is entirely possible to follow a blind course despite healthy eyes. He looked straight at Maria, while the maid, having quickly hidden her face behind the fragile barrier of her hands, reflected, From your mouth to God's ear, Master. Had Enzo known by some chance that happiness betrayed is easily avenged, he wouldn't have ended up where he ended up but would have immediately heeded Mardi's blindness and married the child. She wasn't such a bad catch, if you know what I mean.

But God so desired that that every evening the bishop's courier should arrive, and Mardi should issue orders for his horses to be readied. Several hours later he was received at the Rimini Episcopal headquarters, where he was given this confidential information: Habsburg spies and sycophants were all around, there was a terrible leak of information, anyone might be guilty, and while strengthening all defenses, internal controls should also be redoubled.

Mardi cursed himself and his noble forefathers for leaving him such obligations. But meanwhile in his house a much less uncomfortable scene was taking place. As soon as the master had disappeared from sight, it was as if a breath of freedom wafted through his great home. As was her custom, Catarina gave orders that the guards should raise the Mardi banner upon the main tower. In her understanding this would serve as notification that the master was not at home but that his right hand, which was pictured on the banner as the claw of an incited lynx, still watched over the fate of his subjects. As some clever little head decided, the guards had to be doubled and, upon learning of the beloved master's return, they were to blow all the available trumpets regardless of the time of day or night. Mardi tried to talk Catarina out of at least the night-time trumpeting—"for the world, my dear, is in no way to blame for my return"—but she insisted on this in particular, arguing that her love was stronger even than sleep (this declaration, you understand, comes from an anthology of banalities) and that, whatever happened, she wanted to be awake to greet her one true love, and so on, and so forth.

And on this occasion, as on every other when she was deprived of his company for dinner by some pressing political matter, Catarina gladly abandoned herself to a feeling of neglect. Persuaded by Maria, long before the young Lombardian appeared on her horizon, one similar evening she had allowed the servants to kill time at the master's table. That this had become an established custom by the time of Enzo's arrival was clear from the haste with which the servants rushed through the halls, their extraordinarily elaborate dress, the frequent conversations about the state of Umberto's voice and of his nervous compatriot, for they were excitedly waiting for the Mardi stable boy, should he be in the mood, to rain a hail of punches upon his faithful companion, to everyone's joy and delight.

Well then, all this murmuring, screaming, and shouting woke Enzo from his afternoon slumber. The moment he was up, little Bepo burst into his room with an invitation from the mistress to join her at dinner as soon as he could. After Bepo had announced his message, he rushed to join the treadmill of servants and, in part, gentry, which was, you'll agree with me, an unusual thing and would be even in our time, but Enzo brought him to a stop in the doorway by asking, "Is it always like this here, boy?"

"Only when the old... forgive me, when Master Mardi, is not here, Master Strecci," he answered, bluntly but preciously, which earned him a box on the ear but also, it must be said, a fine silver coin. Bepo concluded that this was truly an exceptional man.

When Enzo entered the dining hall, the company had finished eating what there was to eat, and Umberto had already sung the one about the plum girl and the cowherd, as well as the one about the old master and the young servant girl. The company bowed to him, and Umberto hurried to finish his song, which made him mistake the final lines where the priest says to the harlot in conclusion, "So, sinful soul, take into yourself my Jericho horn with all your heart."

Everyone turned and, after Catarina had introduced him as an important guest, the company as a whole gave him an even warmer welcome.

"You enjoy yourselves thoroughly here, in truth, just as in Milan," began Enzo, but at that moment some obviously tactless soul interrupted him by crying out, "Long live Milan!"

Enzo, however, overlooked the fellow's delight and continued solemnly: "I grew up with servants in my parents' home, which is why I am happy to see such a sight here. Happy servants serving one worth worshiping." With these words he cast a gentle glance upon Catarina, which garnered a sigh from several simple girls from the kitchen, and then the applause resounded. Would that he had known, though he could not, that this gesture took such unpleasant, painful root in Maria's heart, amidst all the wondrous fruit of that garden in bloom for our insanely charming Enzo!

"Pass me that instrument," said the young man, floating on the waves of admiration, and in his hands the lute, usually a noble instrument, became the magical means of emerging adultery, infidelity, betrayal, perversity, crime, and all that is unpleasing to God.

And the lady to whom Enzo sang that evening had, in place of eyes, two suns, hair of life-giving star beams, exactly like our Catarina's, and a complexion paler than milk, exactly like our Catarina's, and two pigeons beneath her gown, and a gait that made one ache, strangely, exactly as our Catarina. The lady was simply a gift from God, but this was not Catarina, for a divine gift would not have come from the devil's lair, as had the gift of her beauty. A divine gift would not make a man want to scream, as our Enzo wanted, and we together with him: *I want her body, even if it should be the last thing I have!*

The final rhymes of that beautiful song evoked another round of applause, and then, tactfully, Enzo excused himself from further participation, saying he was tired. And I can tell you that the adoration that accompanied his departure did not go unnoticed by Catarina.

3

Had my father ordered me as clearly as on the night after the radio broadcast of the Resolution, when he was already exhausted by illness, had he told me to go a fortnight earlier, believe me, I would have obeyed eagerly. Because, in all truth, for an eighteen-year-old Italian boy, from a family of an expelled party member and disempowered partisan, there was no place in the new Yugoslavia. Perhaps for others, those who had managed not to take sides during the war, temporarily turning their backs might have given them the chance of a better life later, but somehow it seemed to me that from the day the regime betrayed my father, the future became for us just a part of his defiance, which at the time, in that room upstairs, had already begun to slowly die out. Besides, a fortnight before the Resolution, I had wanted to be closer to relatives and friends who had already left Rab and who were in refugee camps in the north of Italy.

He made his decision when it was already too late. By then his stubbornness, his firm desire to survive, had made it possible for me to catch a glimpse of her.

It was the middle of June. Our garden, which perched above the road, blossomed with color. Standing in it when the sun began to descend into the lulling night, which was guided by the summer sky and a chorus of crickets, you could see that the house threw a shadow across the whole garden and it seemed as if, compared to the surroundings, it were covered by a dark sheet. At such moments you could see that our house was one of the largest in town, that it could be seen from almost any corner of Rab, while from it, if you wanted, you could make out the little boats in the bay of Saint Euphemia, on one side of town, and the still water of Rab's harbor, on the other.

It had not yet reached that time of day, when she and some of her friends stopped by the fence and began picking blueberries, which were still red and sour. I wouldn't have noticed anything if one of them had not conspiratorially said, "Be careful, those are fascist blueberries." It didn't bother me too much. I was only worried about my father's sleeping. I started off to check on him but then heard one of them make the condemnable, politically dissident statement, "I like them even if they're a hundred percent fascist." The first girl replied that our resolute time would not tolerate such things, but I didn't understand what she meant by it: her answer, us, or the blueberries. I heard her impertinent voice again: "So report me, if you're up to it." This I had to look into: the threads of destiny are forever intertwined.

After having assured myself that my father was sleeping, I went onto the balcony, where my appearance was immediately noticed.

"Death to fascism, Comrade Niccolò," said the first girl in greeting, as was proper for the times though obviously now less belligerent than formerly. I recognized her as Andja, an attractive blond and the leader of Rab's communist youth organization. From everything I'd heard, it seemed to suit her. "Freedom to the people, Andja. How come you don't like my blueberries?"

She lowered her head, blushed slightly, and said, "That's not what I meant, Niccolò. You know how people talk."

"So that means they're good after all," I joked, and Andja laughed in such a way that almost nothing was left of the communist youth leader, and I was happy that my previous playful flirting had yielded some fruit for the sake of duty. But at that moment the rebel spoke: "They're good, very good, even if they are fascist." She stuck her tongue out at me and went slowly off down the road, while Andja saw this as a sign to turn serious.

I decided to find out who the girl was before Andja ran after her friends. "Who's that, Andja?"

"She came from Šibenik the other day. Her name is Petra," she said quickly. "Her father is the new police captain."

And that was the beginning. A funny, completely unimportant encounter, which one might easily forget, you could say. But, you see, that was the rock I would build my destiny upon. Like I said before, destinies intertwined.

Chapter the Third

What is not hidden in the forests of Romagna—such game, such pleasures! Mardi returned home after midnight, with a face that seemed to say that politics was a very hard bread. As a faithful wife, Catarina told him as soon as he came in: "And I'm a hard woman." Francesco thought he knew what she had in mind, so he gave orders to have his horses prepared early the next morning, this time for a hunt. It is important to add that the bishop's words had not allowed him much sleep.

Enzo's first impulse that day was to swear aloud when, at the break of dawn, Umberto's horn cut like a knife into his consciousness. He went to the window and caught sight of Mardi, who seemed to him somewhat absorbed in thought or worried as he waved his banner toward Enzo and then propped it atop his pouch. Not Mardi but Catarina answered the question Enzo had posed, "Where to, my friends, at this time of night?" with the little bit of good will remaining to him.

"Master Strecci," she said, "the sun is about to rise in the east. This is the best time to examine our woods more closely if you wish to."

After these words, which it would be hard for any man to know what to make of, the beautiful Catarina rode away, dragging Mardi and twenty servants still befuddled from the party of the night before behind her.

Enzo caught up with them at the brook that divided the wondrous grove, where the company, gladdened by the morning freshness and the excitement of the hunt, was considering how to surround a family of rabbits. The first thing he made out from the crowd was Maria's charger, which the girl, filled with the strange hope that, regardless of what the mind might be saying, transforms love into drama or, more often, tragedy, turned in his direction. Enzo was able to see her breath curl with every word she so hurriedly sent toward him, the collection of which carried necessary information about the plan for rabbit stew made by Mistress Mardi herself. They could not count on the support of Master Mardi in the mistress's favorite game, for it was clear from the first glance that Master Mardi was absentminded and, in truth, troubled in spirit. Maria accompanied her last sentence with a smile, to which Enzo replied kindly but not especially pleasantly. Maria thought quickly, clearly, and correctly, but, unfortunately, on an unsound foundation, that love needed to be fought for, and she took firm hold of the tail of Enzo's horse, which, it seemed, willingly allowed her to take it as it made its way toward Catarina.

"Dear Enzo," poor Mardi called, "you were all that was lacking to ensure the success of my wife's endeavor."

"Of course, to the fullest and without hesitation," she said in a tone he knew well, accompanying her words with an irresistible movement of the hand so gracefully that a man would be most willing to give up his soul to her, at once and in full consciousness, come hell or high water.

"Leo is my middle name," Enzo responded playfully and, you will agree, rather unoriginally.

"Follow me then," Catarina commanded, and the servants spread out, some on horseback, some with dogs, some on foot, screaming so loudly that the woods shook, and leaving behind old Mardi, who decided to give his soul a rest under a nearby tree.

The sun had just risen above the woods. Catarina raced forward, Enzo spurred his bay, and Maria did not fall a step behind. Catarina flew like an arrow amidst the densely spaced trunks of hundred-year-old trees, while Enzo's nag, whose rider did not allow it to fall behind, felt the danger very well indeed, and even more so did Maria, who did not want to give him the opportunity of slipping away. This unfortunate fact—the fact that, as I said, Catarina was flying headlong in an unknown direction—clearly told the girl that the arranged plan had already largely fallen apart and that some new plan was in effect. Even if she did not understand it clearly, she sensed it all too well in this mad dash.

Catarina suddenly turned aside and was lost amidst the pines, Enzo managed to keep pace with her, and Maria stopped where their horses had left deep tracks. There she sobbed quietly, and for the first time, though without being completely aware of it, grew hateful of her patroness, an unhealthy emotion for a young soul.

Meanwhile Enzo had fallen a good deal behind Catarina. After several minutes of following the hoof tracks and broken branches, he spotted her horse calmly drinking from a small spring. When he approached the water, he spied her washing her neck and face. At that moment he thought of all the things he would gladly sacrifice for this woman, but the list was cut short by her sudden turn. Enzo perceived her surprise when she said, "Ah, it's you. Good.... Why do you look at me so strangely?"

"It seemed to me that you were afraid."

"Believe me, Master Enzo, that fear in this place would be perfectly appropriate. For these woods are filled with bandits of all kinds, and until recently, as my husband revealed to me last night, Habsburg spies. I would not like to see them where you're standing."

"Nor in fact would I be happy meeting them in place of you," Enzo replied, rebuking himself for not thinking of something wittier.

"All the rabbits have fled, as you see. What shall I do now?" she said plaintively.

"Rest a bit. After such a race...."

"Can it be that you are tired, Enzo? Come here, refresh yourself a bit. You didn't notice that we lost Maria?"

What Maria, thought Enzo, as he approached. "No, I really didn't. You led me too far astray, Catarina."

Even before finishing his sentence, he had found her hand. She jumped suddenly away, like some sort of cat, glaring at him in an offended manner, but Enzo did not miss the fact that she had left her hand in his for an impermissibly long time. He took a step back and, bowing his head, apologized, "Forgive me, Catarina. I don't know what came over me. The race must have deprived me of my senses."

Although everything he had said to her after grasping her hand was pure courtliness, as we would say today, Catarina was nevertheless a bit frightened by his last words. She answered cautiously, as cautiously as she was able in such a situation, worried as she was that what seemed to her the overly loud beating of her heart would betray her: "Do not trouble yourself, Enzo. That must be it. The morning air has made you light headed."

She leaped quickly onto her horse and, before dashing away toward the approaching servants, said, "It seems to me that the girl is in love with you. Keep this in mind."

Catarina rode away with the servants, and Enzo trotted toward the tree beneath which old Mardi was sleeping. In all directions the noise of excited hunters and the occasional cry of success could be heard. The upshot of the mistress's hunt was, as usual, hardly enough to satisfy the needs of two healthy adults. But that was not really the reason for going hunting. Here what was being hunted was something concealed beneath the name of Mistress Mardi's good humor. Nevertheless, on this occasion neither the love nor the enthusiasm of the servants could drive away the exhaustion and listlessness of Mardi's wife. It was clear that she was eager to end the game she had started.

While the stable boys were putting a rabbit in a sack, which afforded a moment of rest to the others, Maria uttered to Catarina the bitter words that had swollen up within her like a mountain river, and whose importance the mistress failed to see because of the infatuation taking root within her: "It's as if you are still rushing along with the Lomardian, Madame."

Catarina grudgingly waved her hand, warding off all the advancing poison, and, clenching her teeth, said candidly, "I am tired, Maria. Let us head toward the master."

Meanwhile, Enzo had returned to the place from which the race had begun, sat down next to Mardi, and opened his canteen. Mardi stirred at the harsh odor of brandy and, still half asleep, gladly took the bottle.

"I expect that this will return me my strength, dear Enzo. I'm so beat. And she, by God, it's as if she were living in another world. How do you explain to a woman that the country is at stake?" he said, indicating the seriousness of his work and not concealing a certain pride that performing it afforded him. "I'm too kind. That's why things are like this for me. She knows I would kill for her," he added more softly, looking with affection toward the cloud of dust and listening to the horses' commotion, which made the forest tremble.

"That, I hope, will not happen," said Enzo, comforting both Mardi and himself.

"Well, you never know. But leave off. We must protect ourselves from the Habsburgs. Today I shall announce to the people that we are taking special precautions."

"Is it dangerous? What are we to do?"

"It's so bad that mothers in Rimini bring their children in from the streets as early as five o'clock."

"Five o'clock?" repeated Enzo, clearly disturbed, emphasizing every syllable. "Double the guard, Master."

"I already have," said Mardi, a note of clear satisfaction in his voice. "No one is going to threaten my home, young man."

"But who would dare?" Enzo said, ending the conversation as he took a sip of brandy and recognizing once again all the dear man's simple-mindedness, which offered security and egotism, and he felt himself under some strange protection. But at the same time, Mardi's short speech had breathed fear into his soul: Should he go against himself?

They soon set off for home, having sent little Bepo to take their game quickly to the kitchen once they'd concluded that two bags were enough to carry it all. Bepo carried a few pheasants, rabbits, and wild piglets to the castle to await the master and mistress, the guest, and our maid at table. The tired company dragged itself on; the sun had reached the middle of the sky, and fatigue of differing kinds could be discerned on the faces of Catarina's hunting troop. The Mardis ambled before Enzo, so that he heard Francesco remark upon his wife's pallor and rebuke her with the words, "I told you, darling, hunting is a man's game. Who has ever seen a noblewoman engaged in such labor! This work is not for you. You understand that it's harmful to you. Give it up. Why such stubbornness, my dear ... ," and so on.

And so forth. How boring and senile the old man is, thought two minds in the column, treacherously, at nearly one and the same instant.

4

In the morning, two days after this encounter, I went down to the beach when no one was swimming, in search of at least a little relief from the oppressive heat. I took along a well-known poetry book by Enzo Strecci for added pleasure as I relaxed under a pine tree after my morning swim. These were the poems that he wrote in the days preceding his fall, and it was that morning that I read the verses that just then seemed a proper stimulus for my melancholy. They shall be the motto of my narrative, worth chiseling onto the gravestone under which I shall be placed.

> My inconstant heart one vow alone torments
> That what has come upon me not be forgotten.

It did not take long before someone's hands were suddenly placed over my eyes. I could tell they were a woman's, and the first thing I thought of was that impertinent little creature who so loudly expressed her love for my blueberries. Her thick, dark hair, and that threatening tongue, and those mocking eyes above her slightly Greek nose now appeared in my head as a worthy challenge, and the charm of this vision did not disturb my intense impulse toward deeds that would be pleasing to God.

A wave of heat rushed through my body, and I said, "So my blueberries are good, you think?"

But then the hands quickly fell away and I heard, "Don't be angry, Niccolò, I didn't mean anything by it," and I realized to my disappointment that it was Andja. She moved away, looking at the sea, as if surprised by my question.

"You know how it is. It has to be that way," she added, justifying herself sadly. I wanted to soften her somehow and said, "But how could you possibly malign my blueberries, Andja? Am I the sort of person one can build a young communist career on?"

Such was my attempt, but she did not take up the joke, blushing instead and continuing stubbornly to watch the rippled sea. Then she changed the subject, growing cheerful: "Will you come to the pier today?"

"Maybe," I answered, still thinking about the lovely creature.

"Your friends will be there too?"

She threw a rock away nervously and said, "Why do you ask?" She looked at me from under her brows. "You fancy one of them maybe?"

"No, no. I was just asking."

"So you don't like any of them?" she asked, now trying to outsmart me.

"Well, you're all so pretty."

"But one is prettier to you, right?"

"I can't decide," I said, smiling like a man destined to carry a load he finds sweet, but Andja did not continue the game. She stood up suddenly and appeared almost insulted.

"It's that new girl, isn't it? You like her," she said, and without waiting for an answer, she ran off.

She stopped after several paces and responded, ominously, to the confusion in my eyes, "Watch out for her father. People say he'll stop at nothing when it comes to her."

I took her warning with a sneer and her resentment with the arrogance of an eighteen-year-old youth. Who could know to what extent, but she too had a hand in the misfortune that was about to come upon me. While I walked slowly home, Andja's accusation rang in my ears like a beautiful possibility, like the pleasure of something brand new in a set of familiar, tired out surroundings. And when that something is also irresistible, that much more are the heart and mind nourished with all sorts of often impossible thoughts.

Whether there is something in desire or the devil himself drives us all to the path of ruin, I do not know, but what I had seen in my garden made me think that I had no choice but to give myself up to fate. Approaching the house, I saw the very same blueberry bush moving nervously as if someone was picking berries on the other side. It seemed crazy because I couldn't believe that Ivanka would be gathering them half ripe. I called out her name, but there was no answer. I sneaked into the garden like a thief but was interrupted by a familiar voice.

"Was it Andja again?" I asked the friar impatiently, calling from the chair at the other end of the room, which by now was completely dark.

"If only it had been," he said, pausing. "It was she. I realized it when she spoke."

"They're getting better from day to day," she said. "I don't know about you, but I like sour things. They're not good when they get ripe. It's the sign that their end is near."

"The other day you stuck out your tongue at me, but now you're milling about in my garden," I said, pretending to be cold and unmoved, but in my chest it was as if a small African ensemble was warming up. I was a bit frightened by her impertinence and resolve, and also the courageous way she addressed me. I lowered my eyes for that reason, pretending to pick the overly sour blueberries.

"Am I milling about your heart, too?" she asked, without blinking, while I made a firm decision, at that very moment, not to become confused. "How am I doing in there?" she went on.

"You'll have a tougher time getting there." See how clever and inscrutable I was with her.

"We'll see about that," she said and then approached to within a foot of me. I was as calm as a stone and wouldn't for the life of me have stepped even an inch away. She put a blueberry up to my lips and, holding it there with her finger, moved it slowly across them, as if she was using it to create them again, and then suddenly she put it into her mouth and once again stuck out her tongue at me, this time to show me the whole blueberry on it.

The excitement must have driven all the blood from my face because she laughed loudly and repeated her words. "We'll see about that," she said, backing away. "Hey, meet my father. I followed him here. He's here, upstairs in the house."

"What?!" It struck me, bringing me back from the world of anticipated delight, and I instantly recalled Andja's warning.

"Only sshhh!"

She disappeared behind the fig tree, while I sorted out my thoughts according to Andja's prudent words and tried to imagine the threat that was her father, who, they said, cared dearly about his only daughter, repeating it to myself even after I had realized that I was falling in love and that, like a lover after all, I was prepared to throw caution to the wind. What Petra had said frightened me all the same, but I consoled myself and wondered if this was some new foolishness on her part.

She was telling the truth. In the doorway of my father's room stood Petar Nižetić in the dark blue uniform of a security police commander and, though it was summer, shiny boots up to his knees. His hat was tipped back rakishly, which made his thin, sweat-plastered hair readily visible. He looked all puffy, like an admirer of the loza brandy they made so well in the part of the country from which he had come to us. He stared at me, as a person of power stares, cocking his head mockingly to one side without responding to my greeting until my father, from his bed, said, "This is my son, Comrade Nižetić."

"You don't say! Well look at him, a young man already!"

"He's come to have a talk," said my father by way of introduction since there was no getting anything more from the stranger. "He's the new commander. We've already . . ."

"We're just checking, young man. Just checking. We, Comrade Darsa," he said, turning toward my father, "are watching over you, fallen communists. We know if you're straying farther from the path or, with any luck, improving."

My father passed over these words, lowering his head, and Nižetić turned to me. "How old are you, kid?"

"Eighteen," I answered confidently.

"A little older than my daughter actually."

This seemed to me like a sign of appeasement, like a moment of possible sympathy, so, disobeying her command, I unfortunately blurted out, "I met your daughter the other day at . . ."

I stopped when I saw his sullen expression. Nižetić stepped toward me — Andja was a guardian angel — but stopped just close enough to pat my face, suddenly and somehow gently, with his big, soft palm. A father smilingly offering life advice: "I kill for what's mine, kid. Communism and her." Still smiling, he drew his finger across his neck. "These two are sacred to me. I don't know anything else."

The ensuing silence was broken by Nižetić himself, who was probably satisfied with the effect of its length: "Stay in touch, please. You know where the station is," he said, walking toward the door, and as he stepped out, added, like a guest who has not yet crossed the threshold and whose return is already happily anticipated, "Let us keep each other safe from greater evil, brothers."

Chapter the Fourth

The hunt had exhausted everyone, while the silence during and after the meal stimulated the desire of those present to sink into soft sheets and sleep through the afternoon. Some, in truth, desired to calm their turbulent thoughts. The meal passed quietly. Enzo's kind heart was nevertheless struck by the mistress's silence, which, it seemed, had lasted ever since the scene at the spring. During the entire dinner not a single glance, wince, or gesture came from her direction. Had the morning's encounter been a mere empty fantasy? Had she not left her hand in his too long? He wasn't a child after all, so didn't he know what this meant?

These thoughts of Enzo, which without exaggeration we may call rather melancholic, were interrupted by Mardi, who wanted to inform his intimate circle that he expected them to be present when, within a few hours, from the terrace of the main tower he would warn his subjects of the danger in which they and the whole country found themselves; that is, when he would introduce special security measures across the whole territory of Mardi county, which had the great honor and fortune to be protected from ill fate by his newly incited and, in such a state (he took great pleasure in saying), strikingly resilient lynx.

After Mardi's speechifying, Enzo returned to his spacious chamber rather dejected, in the manner of a gambler after an unsuccessful night. He threw his waistcoat onto the chair, left his hat on the sofa, shoved his boots up to the door of the oak armoire, and listlessly pushed his trousers to the edge of the bed. He sank onto the bed with his full weight, eagerly awaiting the first rays of the peaceful afternoon sun, which would sweep his emerging sadness away, or so he was hoping when, suddenly, he found himself on a horse next to Mardi, embracing him forcefully despite the impediments of the quiver and standard with its familiar lynx. Then he was galloping behind Mardi through a forest at such a speed that all he could see was the glitter of the leaves. Toward what was the honorable duke rushing?

> Our vessel set forth
> After Habsburg spies,
> Oh, he who does not swear or curse
> Will perish in the bishop's chains ....

And while the song echoed all around, Enzo saw Catarina approaching from one side, aiming her bow menacingly at them. Mardi laughed as if he were on his way to a wedding, truly, as if he were not even threatened by her obvious insanity. And she released an arrow that struck Enzo below his chest. He saw from her tears and furious destruction of the bow that he had not really been the target, but that learning how to hunt is not easy. Mardi saw what had happened, took out his own dagger, and thrust it into Enzo's body just below the first wound, from which much blood was already flowing.

Enzo jumped up in a cold sweat and put his hand to the wounded place. The sight of his own room calmed him, but just in case he tested the spot that had just before been an excruciating puncture. But instead of torn flesh and blood, he felt there the sharp edges of a folded paper, and, turning it over, noticed a single, ornate "M" on the back. Here is what was inside:

Maria's letter:

> *From the moment my eyes caught sight of you, they have seen nothing else, nothing except you, and you know it. You could subject me to ridicule, and I would put up with it, if you were mine. You could squash my heart with your boot—oh, what more than this letter do you need?—and it would still beat, if you were mine. For this I am willing to be punished, willing to leave everything behind. Why are you cruel? Why do you torment me? Today when you came toward me in the woods, I saw your smile. I need no other confirmation of your love. If you don't know your own heart, so be it. I have seen into it! Why did you want to make me jealous when you galloped after Milady? Are my tears so dear to you? If so, only say yes and you'll receive them beyond measure! Why do you not admit to whom you sang last night? To whom if not to me? As I write you these lines, my heart wants to explode. Now everything depends upon you. Oh,*

must I repeat that I would live with you even in a
dungeon, in chains, with my leg crushed in a Spanish
boot? Only, remember, if you'll be mine.

Needless to say,
love,

Maria

Enzo read the final (highly stylized) words and did not know what to think or where to turn. Sleep-drunk as he was after the nightmare during which his beloved Catarina had mistakenly shot an arrow through his ribs, and Mardi, glowing with happiness, had put his dagger to the test, this letter, which mentioned jealousy and song, and which threatened torture and imprisonment, disturbed him to such a degree that he angrily tore it into tiny pieces. And while the scraps were still sailing about the room, he exclaimed, exhausted: "Is somebody making fun of me? What does that girl want from me?! What 'ridicule'? What 'heart'? What 'proofs'? Whose 'jealousy'?! What does 'needless to say' mean? In God's name, what 'dungeons and chains,' damnit?! Someone around here is completely insane.

5

What else could I do but avoid her? I tried not to go out. I chose deserted places for swimming. I did all this and, of course, couldn't stop thinking about her.

I was actually waiting for an encounter like the one in the garden. I hoped she would run into me in such a place where—what's the use, let's be a little banal—I wrote her name in the sand, left coded messages on trees, believed in the compatibility of souls, was sad when she didn't appear for meetings to which I hadn't invited her. In short, I was in love: I took a single sign as inevitable destiny; I was prepared to suffer. And, of course, I enjoyed it a little. You're smiling, Bosnian, but is there anyone who hasn't gone through it at least once in his life? If there is, then, as the Teacher would have said, he is more like an animal or some kind of deity.

The end of June drew near, bringing great events with it. While the representatives of the Central Committee of the Communist Party were gathered somewhere in Romania, our representatives having been excluded, which marked the beginning of the age of new victims, I tried to preserve my heart from devastation, or so it seemed to me, to defend my own interests, and, to be completely honest, I didn't really give a fig. The only thing that occasionally calmed me down was my father coughing in the night, but, hearing him breathing again, I would return to the world of a twosome of fantastic pleasures.

I displayed particular courage by walking under her window several times each day, hoping for a sign from her, without daring to leave off or, God forbid, toss a pebble. Yes, yes, my heart and mind were aching, so I decided to look for her among the Communist Youth.

It was the twenty-eighth of June of forty-eight. Every man has a day that's like a fulcrum for a lever that overturns all his previous life. That day was my fulcrum. The man sitting before you and to whom you've been listening all this afternoon and evening is the product of it.

I learned that her father had kept her locked up at home ever since he'd paid us that strange family visit. Again it was Andja, who else, that told me. I ran into her around noon on the stage of the People's Hall, where she was in charge of hanging banners and decorating the interior for the upcoming celebration of the Day of Revolt. She wasn't laughing like before. She seemed a little put off, probably because of our last meeting. As I said before, I was in love and didn't much care about other people's feelings. That's why I was too quick to ask her about Petra, which gave her the chance to get me back for my previous barbs.

She understood what was on my mind and toyed with me. "So you're in love with her, what do you know?!"

I defended myself as if admitting she was right would cost me my head.

She remarked on it, and then, seeing my unambiguous silence, added maliciously, "Maybe it will, who knows? Besides, none other than Commander Nižetić asked me about you."

I stood my ground. "And what did you tell him?"

"What every girl in this town knows," she laughed, hesitating, "that you're ... dangerous. And ..."

"And what?" I asked, my nerves on edge.

"Well, that you've been asking about her."

"But I haven't ..." I began, defending myself clumsily.

"You said you liked her, and now you're scared. Well, Comrade Niccolò, we have been taught to live up to our responsibilities. And as for who's responsible and who's not, our commander knows best, which is why he's keeping her locked up. Because there are *subversives* on the loose."

She looked at me as if she wanted to brand the word into my forehead. I started to snap back but then decided all at once to leave her presence and never set eyes on the creature again. It seemed to me then that she not only heralded misfortune, she incited it.

However, as the poet says, we search everywhere for what we lack, and therefore I set off for home, and that's where she was. Tormented by Andja's malice, I found her waiting for me on the veranda. When I got there, she was talking with Ivanka. The surprise of seeing her was enough to make everything inside me burst into flame.

She saw me and exclaimed, "I've been waiting for you a whole hour, Niccolò, you naughty boy!"

I was disturbed by the bruise under her right eye, which prompted her to respond, almost proudly, "I earned this on your account."

Ivanka ducked into the kitchen. I sat down next to her. I didn't know what to say. She took my hand and ran my fingers over the purple skin beneath her eye. It was as if my hand wiped all the confidence from her face. It seemed the right moment to kiss her, but when I moved my lips closer, she pulled away.

"Sorry. I don't know what came over me," I said, downcast.

"It must have been me," she said, and it seemed her answer brought her to her senses as she asked, pretending to be scared, "Or maybe it wasn't?"

Again she was the sweet demon. I lowered my eyes. She asked me to walk her at least part of the way home. She added that her father had been at work since morning and that he had something serious to take care of, so we had nothing to be afraid of. I followed her, for an invitation from her easily led back to the path of misfortune.

I started off in front of her, pretending to be offended by her game. She took my hand in the middle of the street. It was clear I was defenseless against that.

Soon a man on a bicycle passed us.

"That's my father's snitch. That guy never leaves anything to chance," she said, almost admiring her father's cunning. She waved at the man on the bicycle when he turned to make sure it was her, and laughed at my discomfort.

"He'll stop you from going out again," I said seriously, but she didn't like where the conversation was going, so she suddenly stopped.

"You love me, Niccolò?" She tried to look into my eyes, but I was so confused that I didn't know what to do, what to say. Two sets of feelings were mixed together inside me—outrage that made me reject her and infatuation that made me desire her. I wanted to torture her and embrace her at one and the same time. I didn't know where to begin, even without knowing that I wouldn't have the chance to do so, because at that very moment Nižetić came around the corner, out of breath and obviously informed, and rushed at us.

He grabbed her by the hand and shoved her to the side. He seized me by my shirt and took a swing, but her scream stopped him. Before pushing me to the ground, he merely said, "Stalin betrayed us, kid, and you're playing with your life. Get lost, or you're fucked."

I lay in the dust, helplessly watching him drag her away. And then she suddenly broke free and shouted to me, "Yes or no?!"

I didn't say anything because I could no longer hear or see anything: I was running away as fast as I could. I hid in somebody's back yard, calming myself and waiting to gather my courage before heading home. I could not show up before my sick father in that state.

Chapter the Fifth

Worthy people!
The enemy is at the gates. The herds at our borders no longer
graze in peace. The hands of outsiders harvest our grain. Soldiers
dig trenches in our fields. Why is this so?
Ever since Lombardy fell into Habsburg hands, the north of
our country has been under threat, and our enemy's ruthless greed
has been aimed at us. In the name of the bishop, I warn you
that our homeland is in danger. According to the most reliable
sources, Habsburg spies are everywhere, perhaps even amongst you
at this very moment. Believe it or not, they could be anyone. It
is your duty to report any suspicious person, anyone coming into
our country from the north, be he even your relative or a good
tradesman. We shall triple the guard. All able-bodied men in their
right mind are obliged to report to the nearest garrison, and every
household is hereby required to pay one quarter of its possessions to
Rimini's episcopal treasury, for the sake of our country's defense and
our children's future, which is, as we all know, the first and most
essential thing for every honest heart . . . .

*

While Mardi spoke to the assembled multitude, Catarina stood one step behind her husband. Enzo, as an important guest, stood to her right, and the maid, as always, two paces behind her mistress. On Enzo's way to the main tower, Maria had intercepted him in a corridor and greeted him politely, but he had merely smiled, bowed, and continued on his way in the belief that it was for the best and that, in the end, she would cool down.

But his cold response made Maria think that perhaps the letter had slipped beneath his bed or that a gust of wind had blown it far from his sight, so she decided to investigate the matter when the occasion should present itself, or write a new letter, which would not have been a hardship for her.

As the crowd's cries of bewilderment turned to belligerent chanting, and the sound of the drums furnished Mardi's words with a magnificent background, Enzo attempted to touch Catarina with the side of his body, several times succeeding, while Catarina responded in a slightly more welcoming manner than she had after the hunt. Behind the sweaty back of Mardi, whose heart and throat were swollen with praise of the homeland, and for whom the people cheered excitedly, thereby confirming the everlasting value of old, never-fading clichés, Catarina avoided Enzo's hand, looking with steadfast grace upon the masses. Only when the crowd expressed its noisy approval did they have the chance to exchange a phrase or two. Maria caught their whispers, and jealousy gripped her heart. It is important to keep in mind, so that you understand where we are in the story, that Enzo's persistence in these moments could no longer be justified by shortness of breath or the fresh morning air or anything of the sort: no holds were barred now.

At the moment he squeezed her hand, Catarina hissed, "You would betray such a man? You would forsake his hospitality?" "As God is my witness, I would follow that man to the ends of the earth. As God is my witness, Catarina, my soul loves all that is his. As God is the witness of my torment and love, which knows no words, heeds no explanation, seeks no consent," whispered Enzo while with his thumb and forefinger he took hold of the wedding ring on her right hand and reached as far as the gold-studded green diamond crafted in Anvers or Antwerp. This caused Catarina to pull back somewhat, as if it had suddenly become clear what she was letting herself into, and Enzo, understanding what was happening, went on quickly: "Tell me, do you want me to leave? There, set your husband on me. Throw me out of your home.... By handing me over to his dogs, you would be saving my soul. But keep in mind," said Enzo, the sweet-tongued prince, after a short pause, "this love will continue to tear my breast apart even when the last bits of me have vanished from your world. Tell me if that's what you want, and I'll be gone by the time the sun completes its day's journey. I've given myself up to you—the decision is yours."

His last words seemed somehow familiar to him, but he came to his senses when her ring nearly slipped from her finger. All but petrified with fear, Catarina abruptly pushed away his hand for the second time that day.

"That's enough now," she said too loudly, so that old Mardi turned to his wife, indicating by his smile to be patient a bit longer.

6

He was sitting up in bed when I came in. You could hear the news from the radio, which was lit by two candles, and which gave his features an even more ghostly look than usual. I washed up, letting the water drip from my face.

"See what's happening, Niccolò? Now they'll turn on us," he said, his voice sad. It did not bring me back to my usual self.

I didn't comprehend what he was saying. I thought he was upsetting himself over nothing again.

"It's time for you to leave," he said. "You must go to Italy, Niccolò. We have no future here."

When I said that we'd go together or not at all, that I wouldn't go anywhere without him, he ordered me to sit on the bed. He didn't get angry as he normally would have. He repeated once again what he had said before, asking if I'd seen what was happening around us, and so on, as if to bring me back to my senses. He was dying, and I was thinking about her.

"My days are numbered, Niccolò. I don't have much time left. You mustn't stay here. They're going to attack us. Don't you understand that they need scapegoats now?"

He asked me to bring him a pillow. His face was that of a man who had lost his battle with life, a man who had only enough strength left to sow the seeds of a wish or two for the future. He held my hand as if to keep me from running away while he still had the strength to speak. It was the first time in my life that I really feared losing my father. I cried in his lap like a little child, for both of us.

"You must leave with the exiles, the *esuli*," he began, "There will be no one left to look after you when I die. You have nothing to stay here for. You're not me. I had a dream to follow. Your dream is still out there, waiting for you wherever you go."

Never before until that day, that night of revelations, had I understood his despair. His attempt to convince me to leave was the attempt of a man who believed that one's last words were sacred and that they should be respected because of the memory of the deceased. But who among us was ever ready to accept such words, to take seriously the death that would confirm them? That would be a betrayal of the loved one after all.

"You see, when Mussolini's troops occupied this place," he said, "I made a vow to myself. Maybe it was irrational, but it was certainly human. Down there, under our fig tree I buried a small barrel. Inside it, Niccolò, I placed our flag. I planned to open it and place it on the top of our house once we had attained our freedom. After four years of war, when we finally won out, I was so happy that I completely forgot about it. But I remembered it one night, sleepless like many others before now, not long after they had expelled me from the party. I found myself looking at the fig tree under which I had buried it, and realized I was crying just like you're crying now. I turned into an exhausted and lonely man, hunched atop my own life's work, as it were, and that hole seemed to me like the grave the convict has dug for himself with his own hands. Only unlike me the convict can console himself because whatever might befall him will not happen by his own will but by someone else's. I found it hard to think about that stupid barrel under the fig tree. The image explained my situation to me perfectly. That flag in the barrel seemed to me like a treasure buried in the ground, Niccolò, a treasure we would never unearth."

Such were my father's words. He seemed unable to continue. He shook his head and licked his dry lips. He lifted me from his lap and only managed to add, serenely, that the following evening, at ten o'clock, I would be taking the ship for Trieste. He left no room for disagreement. He was now a completely gentle man. There was no trace of his former fighting spirit and inflexibility. His illness had dried everything up in him.

After his speech, he could do little more than collapse. He wiped my tears and patted my wet cheek. Then he lowered his hand as if it too had become a burden to him.

Chapter the Sixth

Right. All right then. So now what? Everything's clear. Hide and seek's over. What next? When the future depends on the will of a woman, it's uncertain, isn't it? Should I lie low? Should I press on? If I abandon everything, the insult might make her do something rash. Then again, take the bull by the horns.... Such were the thoughts of Enzo, his mind whirling. *Some things bode well, but be honest, you still don't know anything for sure. If only something could take us into the clear, one way or another.*

In less than the turning of a smallish hourglass, not two hours since old Mardi, now out recruiting soldiers in the county, had given his great speech, little Bepo, letter in hand, knocked on Enzo's door. Enzo snatched the letter from him angrily, thinking that the maid must have decided to operate in the open now, through the servants—a malicious and oft-exercised practice typical of her class, designed to influence public opinion behind his back and without his knowledge, in short, to force him to do something hasty, expose him to public pressure—but then he realized that Bepo had jumped aside after the letter's violent removal and that he was not moving from the spot, as if he expected a blow and wanted to reduce its effect.

The first thing that came to Enzo's mind was, for purely pedagogical reasons, to let his hand express his inner state, but then he recalled the delicacy of the matter at hand and, in the belief that people should be brought to their senses (and to his side) through peaceful means, pulled out a silver coin in answer to Bepo's hopes.

"This time without effort or ornament, eh?" he said aloud, distractedly turning the white bundle over in his hands once he had closed the door. But the mere sight of the handwriting told him that no servant was behind it.

It was her message, by God. This was the lever he had waited for. His hope rose up like a pile of dust stirred by a fierce breeze. Now you be the judge of whether something had come into the clear.

Catarina's message:

This has gone too far. You ruined my hunt. You spoiled the pleasure of listening to the important speech of gentle Francesco, my husband. You upset my evening hours. Why have you done this? Since I do not have time to wait for your reply, because the previous question is not a mere order required by rhetoric, I want you to know that I see very clearly that similar things (that is, destruction, ruin, anxiety) will continue in the future. I will not allow you to do this! Which is why I ask you, and you have done me too much wrong not to obey: keep the contents of this letter secret (do not object—Bepo does not know how to read) and follow my instructions. First, when my husband disappears from sight, due to pressing political matters, and when the banner is raised upon the main tower, wait until the clamor in the corridors dies somewhat, then hurry to my chambers. This should be enough for you. You understand we must discuss this matter. It is only thanks to the goodness of my heart that I feel compelled to give you yet another chance.

Catarina Mardi

Oh, how long were those days of counting the hours of boredom and anticipation of the moment of Mardi's political engagement, that incited lynx whose claws at last stretched forth once the trouble had come to his land! They had a hard time of it, all four of them. Closed in their chambers and secretive about their intentions, they descended only at meal times into the dark dining room, which, because of the heavy clouds that had poured rain onto the country for days on end, they lit up with heavy candles from Assisi.

The master wrote letters and awaited replies. The communication lines with Rimini were kept open at all times, even when the road became blocked by a landslide, which Mardi's messenger came upon one morning. It had to be cleared immediately, so Enzo himself had taken part. That was the only event of those days that drew him forth from his bed and his room, in which, inspired by the hysteria of waiting for love and by doubts that bring on pain and excitement, he composed a kind of legacy in verse, which would later make him famous.

During that time, Catarina kept Maria close, and the two of them very often secluded themselves in Catarina's chambers, which seemed to Mardi unnecessary and childish and which Catarina justified by saying that, thank God, love problems that pressed upon the honest girl required her help. We shall never cease to be amazed at the happy confusion in which Mardi and his wife's maid lived.

Because of the numbness of social life the rain forced upon them all, which is to say, because it was impossible for her (or, it needn't be forgotten, her mistress) to meet Enzo frequently, Maria forgot all about her previous jealousy. Incited by her insane heart, she talked excitedly to Catarina for hours about his mornings, his habits, his walks across the castle, and the secret writing to which he devoted himself completely.

I tell you there's nothing strange in all this, Bosnian. Who could ask for more than to witness, daily, the wondrous effect your soul has on the person by your side? To see that your every thought and word are clear proof of the constant presence of desire, hers open, yours thinly disguised? And considering all this, need I say it again, it's not surprising to fall in love with that which those closest to you love most, is it? Is there anything more natural? And is there anything more normal than being afraid that someone might snatch away that which has taken root in your heart?

7

The next afternoon, while packing my bags to go, I was interrupted by an announcement over the town's public address system. Every few minutes it called the public to a meeting in front of the Rector's Palace, and through the window I could see young men with banners hurrying down the street. A song was audible; children came running, along with women and old people who had left their work to hear the officials. It was, I believed, my last day among these people, and I wanted to join them. Actually, I yearned to see her and was hoping to get an answer.

For nearly ten minutes I stood amidst the mass of people under the balcony of the Rector's Palace, waiting with the others for Petar Nižetić's speech. I thought she would have to be somewhere in the crowd. I looked for her like a madman, pushing my way through the gathered townsfolk. I finally gave up and, still painfully aware of last night's confrontation, found a place at some distance from the balcony behind a tall man.

I was struck by the fact that I hadn't seen any pictures of Stalin on my way to the square. Nor were there any banners with his name on them. White patches along the walls of buildings now poorly covered the signs of a bygone era, over which, almost without warning, a veil of lime had fallen the night before.

The clamor of the crowd grew louder. The kolo dance spun round. Battle songs memorialized in song books from the war rang out. Nižetić, like a good director, had arranged things so that the moment this joy began to abate, he should appear on the balcony, which was supported by two famous lion's heads, and from which important pronouncements had been delivered to the people of Rab for centuries.

On the wall behind him someone had displayed the national flag, and before turning to the assembled people, Nižetić saluted it resolutely. Then, all tucked in and dressed up, he positioned his immense body in front of the flag's star, as if to make it clear who was the foremost defender of the homeland and spokesman on its behalf.

The friar climbed onto the chair he'd been sitting in and stood there like an orator, imitating Nižetić. He winked at me, then glanced around the whole room, gesturing for quiet to the imaginary audience.

All grew quiet, and he began:

Comrades!

Why are your vineyards empty, and why do hoes lie abandoned in your fields? Why are our nets, comrade fishermen, spread out along the jetty?

A dark shadow has fallen upon the homeland from a place where, until yesterday, we saw only light. Thence comes the enemy, who has sent tanks against our small country with the sole desire of destroying the freedom of our people, won through the price of

our blood. But we won't be placed under anyone's heel, comrades!
We won't allow them to do it! (That's right! Applause. Vehement
cheering. Comrade Tito! Nižetić's gesture for the singing to
stop. Silence.)
The homeland is threatened. Our inheritance is in danger!
But our freedom, which annoys our enemies, only we can defend!
(From the audience: Long live comrade Tito! Long live Tito!
Applause, again some begin to sing, but Nižetić, growing more
nervous, cuts it short with an abrupt motion of his arm before
it can be taken up by the crowd and disturb his planned course
of speech.)
Under the leadership of comrade Tito, we are ready to defend
our country again, at all costs, and to the last man. Are we ready?
(The crowd answers: Yes!)
But you are mistaken if you believe that everyone thinks as you
do. Remnants of the past may still be seen among us, in those
who have not embraced the new order, and who would gladly pass
judgment upon our young state. Who are they, you wonder? (A
pause. Complete silence.) *All those, comrades, who avoid working*
in our communal fields during the day and listen to radio London
and Moscow at night! (Nižetić gave special emphasis to the last
two words and then stopped, upon which everyone grew quiet,
and tension and bewilderment took hold of the assembly.)
The imperialist politics of the Soviet Union have positioned its
war machinery on our borders to destroy the fruits of our people's
struggle. Yesterday they were still our brothers, but today, driven
by their selfish goals, they have abandoned the political course long
ago charted by comrade Lenin and turned their backs upon our
homeland. But never a slave! (And that was the real signal for
the crowd to begin chanting from all directions: *Better the grave*
than a slave!)

Nižetić grinned and shouted loudly and clearly, *Down with Russian imperialism and its servants! Long live comrade Tito!* (This caused enormous delight, which lasted for some time, while the brass band began to play and the kolo dance formed again. But Nižetić's serene figure made it clear to the gathered multitude that he had not yet finished, so the crowd obediently quieted again.)

I have told you about their servants, comrades. They are among us, comrades. They sit at your dinner table. They coil around your children like snakes and plot your downfall. For that reason, for the cause of public security, it is the duty of all who carry the homeland in their hearts and the work of comrade Tito in their heads to report anything they know about any suspicious case, any suspicious person, for no one is safe anymore, dear comrades. (This seemed to stun the crowd). *No one!*

But is vigilance enough? Is it enough to just say it? Is it enough to just pledge oneself? Well, to that I tell you definitely not! The homeland demands actions! Actions, comrades! Let every ablebodied man report to the people's authority for placement. Let every household deposit a portion of its belongings in the communal center! Let the work schedule on communal fields be increased! And let numerous other measures be undertaken, for that is the only way to defend the homeland's fortunes. For that is the only way to build the future of our children. For that, comrades, is the only way to stand firmly behind the words of comrade Tito delivered at the Neretva: We shall defend the sun of our freedom! And so, long live comrade Tito!

Nižetić's firmness enjoyed unbelievable success. The crowd seemed to boil over. Again the band took up its refrain, flags were unfurled, and, from the back rows, through all the slogans and cheering came that same song, now much more resolutely than when Nižetić had managed to silence it, which he readily took up now, the megaphone pressed to his lips. It looked as if the celebration would continue well into the night.

The friar got down from the chair and sat on it. I laughed at his performance.

Yes, it was dramatic, he responded. I barely made it out of that crowd. I headed for home. I had to finish packing, kiss my father good-bye, and leave my home behind. I couldn't stop thinking about her. The weight of what I was leaving behind made me sit down on the wall edging the road and plunge my head into my hands. My sadness, fed by not having met her, was suddenly transformed into rash courage. A fateful idea crossed my mind, and I embraced it readily and without thinking. I nearly cried out with joy. Soon the quick blossoming of my thought filled the empty streets that led to her house, and when I think back on it today, I realize there was nothing to be done about it, for the wheel of my destiny was spinning ever faster—with the support of all my heart.

An act of God must have kept me from looking behind me. I was later to learn that (my subsequent story will make it clear that I do not exaggerate) my personal downfall was hounding my tracks just then.

The silence surrounding Petra's house gave me courage, and I knocked eagerly. She appeared at the window and stood still, like a frightened pigeon. She recovered quickly, the expression of surprise vanished from her face, and she repeated in her familiar voice, "So is it yes or no?"

She did not wait for my answer but, a few seconds later, opened the door and hurriedly pulled me inside.

"So it's yes after all," she said, for the first time without hiding her excitement, and, believe me, I didn't have to say anything. She kissed me and impatiently removed my clothes as if she had been planning it for a long time, as if she knew every little part of my body. I unfastened her buttons, and her breasts fell from her blouse, and I plunged my face into them. She drew me into her room, and that whole afternoon the sounds of song and the murmur of the crowd floated in from outside, creating, we believed, a veil protecting our union. Night approached slowly from the east, and now I understand that all that was just dream and delirium. False belief in the favor of destiny, blindness, infatuation with happiness, which we thought had come to stay for good, but which, oh, as I would soon discover, was tailored by Petar Nižetić, who had sent his spies after me. I didn't have the strength to tell her I was leaving. I let the role of happiness, rare and perhaps unique in my life, run its course.

Only after we heard the footsteps of the people coming home from the ceremonies did we understand that the end was drawing near: she thought it was for that night only; I was convinced it was for good.

Still, overcome by the sadness of departure and regrets about my silence, I revealed to her a part of what my father had told me the night before, leaving out his order. At the door that opened onto her garden and led, beyond that, to my house, where my father waited anxiously for me, I told her the story about the flag, about our happiness, call it what you will. At the end I added, ominously, that it was the flag that would cover our corpses.

In place of a response, she kissed me gently on the forehead, as if she were calming a child, and then, hopeful and smiling, she added, "Don't you think ours is already flying?"

Chapter the Seventh

That state of deceptive stillness, even on the surface of unseen motion, amidst turmoil and momentous decisions, when a man often allows his thoughts to give him pause before the window or with his head sunk into a pillow; that state in which those closest to us are not, shall we say, the most important to us (let alone their concern for our behavior); that state which is merely cautious composure came to an end early in the evening five days after the first drops of rain were noted on the castle windows, and here again the bishop of Rimini spurs along our story by inviting Mardi to an urgent night-time assembly.

Do you think that Enzo, having heard the trumpets announcing Mardi's departure, patiently waited for the standard to be raised, the corridors to grow quiet, and the crowd to disperse, as Catarina had clearly instructed him? Oh no. He was so exhausted in all these days—with his forced peace and solitude, which aided his writing and also made him feel the need for a supportive voice—and burdened by all the implications of her message—which, contrary to what you might expect, dispelled all his feeble thoughts and strengthened his resolve and the rhythm of his heart, for everything was about her, everything in him waited impatiently for the standard to be raised—he was so exhausted, I say, that he left his chambers the moment that Maria, taking advantage of the commotion and a request from Catarina, and driven by infatuated hope and optimism, appeared in his corridor. After giving the order for the standard to be raised, Catarina expressed to Maria her desire not to be disturbed in the coming hours, excusing her absence from dinner, and any possible entertainment, on the pretext of a sudden headache. Maria mistakenly took this as an opportune moment to visit Enzo without hindrance or, should he not be there, at least leave him a new letter, and she hurried toward him. When she reached the corridor, she caught sight of Enzo going down it in the other direction, which, given the melancholy of his past several days, struck her as rather strange. This sudden transfiguration, this hurried departure counseled her to discover where the man was going.

Enzo rushed down the corridor and soon found himself in the most beautiful part of the castle, the master wing. The placement of dignitaries' portraits indicated the growth and offshoots of the Mardi pedigree. He was amazed by the grandeur of their brave leaps over obstacles on horseback (their faces turned to the artist), and of their upright posture beside the family coat of arms, a cross above their heads, children atop their knees, one hand caressing a spouse's head, and he who had prepared himself for a thief's ill-deed was stung by their stern glances. He shuddered. Soon the excitement that had caused a lump to form in his throat began to give way before what he only now realized was the vagueness of the message: which door should he knock on?

Enzo continued on and, after stopping and putting an ear to some of them, spotted an almost invisible pink veil before one, which marked the entrance to her private chambers, intended for repose from the world. He lifted the veil from the floor and went inside; and had he, at that moment, looked back down the corridor, perhaps he would have noticed Maria peering around the corner, and, who knows, perhaps that would have saved him.

The room was dark. Nothing could be heard. For a moment he thought he was mistaken. But soon he caught sight of a figure by the window and impatience took hold of him. "Here I am," he whispered.

"Did anyone see you?" interrupted Catarina abruptly.

"I don't think so," he stuttered.

"Don't think! Do you realize what I'm risking by meeting you like this, Enzo?" Her tone frightened him somewhat, but her intimate use of his name encouraged him. His eyes were growing used to the darkness, and, though she tried to calm the shaking of her voice, she seemed to be trembling. "Do you understand?" she repeated. "You well know why I asked you here. It's clear to you that you did something unacceptable ...." She broke off as if she was out of breath.

He finally conquered his fear and approached resolutely to within a few paces of her, close enough to sense that on this evening her beauty found itself in the most favorable conditions for displaying all its power. He was overcome by the immobility one feels upon meeting something long sought after, that silent tension of the body which, before we take the object into our hands, forces us to let seconds go by, as if every passing second increases its value. The rapid movement of her breast, her figure shining in outline as she leaned against the background provided by the window, her face beneath the dark veil, her lips whose contours could be seen only when she turned her head to one side, her words of caution... oh Lord, it was worth the wait.

"Come no closer. That is close enough for us to hear each other well. Even very well. As I told you, there are many things we must discuss. You cannot, Enzo... because of everything...."

"Order me to leave, Catarina. Bring this miserable presence in your shadow to an end. Expel him who stands in the way of your happiness. It will be better for us both...."

"Silence. Do not say such things, Enzo. God hears all." She paused as he took another step. "Don't make me...," she began but broke off and closed her eyes. She realized that she had lost all sense of confidence, that what she had wanted to say had flown away irretrievably, like a veil in the wind, that she was losing herself amidst Enzo's ever strengthening scent.

That, in short, it was too late she understood once she opened her eyes. No longer could she order him to back away. No longer could she utter his name. Or bring the two of them to their senses.

8

The friar paused after his final words, as if he lacked the strength to go on.

"You went back after all," I said.

"You're a good listener, I see. Yes, I went back from Trieste, right into the hands of my enemies. Only a few days had passed since the night of my departure from Rab, and there I stood on the ship deck looking at my hometown, our four cathedral towers, the outline of the Church of St. John the Evangelist and St. Mary's, the Rector's Palace and Dominis-Nimira Palace as well as the walls of St. Andrew Monastery. All this meant I was home. I remember a strange fever coming over me, a strange homecoming joy. I thought about her and expected much. Still, my thoughts were merely a product of suffering then, the warped optics of a man in love. Yes, only a couple of days had passed since the Resolution and the heat that came down on us was a warning from God, my friend."

From the moment I stepped onto the town quay, I considered what my father might say, his anger, and how I could defend myself. I believed that our love, Petra's and mine, was still a secret, that I had nothing to be afraid of, and that I had returned to begin living my real life. I passed through Rab's streets slowly, taking my time on my way home. I felt excited, and my excitement in the midst of the peaceful town seemed to me like a torch on a dark, clear night. The thought seduced me completely, and I felt at home amidst the island's late-afternoon landscape. There was no sign of what was to befall me just a few paces ahead.

A little over an hour had passed since my arrival, and I decided to go home. But that had been enough time for the news to reach my persecutors. I remember being surprised to see a man in a blue uniform run across the end of St. Jerome Street, covering the distance in two or three hops. At that moment, as if some dark premonition had crept into my lungs, my breathing became terribly heavy. But I went on and, just at the spot where the man had skipped across, felt a strong blow on my back, upon which I blacked out.

The next thing I saw was my father's face. When I realized he was standing over me, it seemed to me that I had never left the house where I was born. It was obvious his strength was ebbing because he was hardly able to pat my head wordlessly. In that delirium I had a false sense that I was under his roof, which for a brief moment filled me with delight, but as I tried to get up I felt pain in my shoulder and neck. The ceiling filled with angels, which I had just begun to make out, and my father's first words were enough to dash all my hopes.

"Just tell me what made you come back? I've been waiting for you to wake up and thinking of nothing but that. What made you come back?"

I raised my head and saw we were not alone. Seven more people were crammed with the two of us into that small room with angels painted on its walls. I knew some of them. I will not tell you their story because that would take us too far afield, and yet it would amount to the same—that the new government had something against them. I turned around and saw the barred windows, and all my doubts about my present condition were cleared away by the uniformed man who peered in through the small window of the heavy wooden door. But where were we?

"At the Benedictine monastery, next to St. Andrew's," said one of the men arrested with us under, they explained, the same accusation.

My father, they said, was the leader of the Cominform rebellion on the island. I was his accomplice. Three farmers from the inland were informers. And the four Italians, including the two of us, were agents of the Italian Communist Party. Such was the indictment according to which they were all arrested a day after my departure. My departure to Italy was taken as strong evidence for the indictment against my father. He told me that we were facing imprisonment and perhaps even death. I hugged him and wept. In response, he only managed to ask, "Niccolò, what made you come back here?"

He looked consumed from the inside. His pallor and dryness showed unmistakably that he was near death, and seeing him like that I was overwhelmed by embarrassment over my reason. So I said nothing. My foolish return enabled me to spend only two days more with him, and to play a part in the journey he took, his sudden death, as silent as that of a fish.

Some time before evening Niżetić entered the room. Deftly twisting the nightstick in his hands, he stood at the door, obviously pleased with the effect, and said, "What's up, birdies? Feel better now that you're not alone, eh? You, kid, you're coming with me. This is the end for you, this time."

I started walking toward the door, but before I walked out, his stick stopped me, and he said, "What did I tell you? You're fucked or I'm not Petar Niżetić."

I passed through the long monastery corridor, and the guard, whom I would owe my life to, followed. Officiously, without saying a word, he walked behind me to the first turn. When we were alone in the staircase leading to the basement, he asked, "Is your name Darsa?"

"Niccolò Darsa," I replied without turning.

"Just making sure you're the same guy who shared a desk with me in school," he said, then laughed and stopped in the middle of the corridor, waiting for me to stop and turn. There was no doubt. It was Ivan Mršić, the son of a farmer from the island's interior, with whom I'd attended the first grades of the improvised communist partisan secondary school. I hadn't recognized him under his cap and his police uniform. I was so happy I almost jumped on him, but suddenly he pointed his bayonet at me and shouted, "Move on, you treasonous scum!"

The order echoed through the corridor and I had no choice but to turn away, which is when I saw a police lieutenant coming from the basement:

"Carry on, Mršić, carry on! Don't give the bandits any peace!" he said as he passed.

*

We went on in silence to a narrow basement room, where I was supposed to wait for Nižetić. Mršić made me sit on a chair, then positioned himself, out of precaution, at the door. "I was with them when we were arresting your father," he said, "and when we followed you around town. They almost picked me to smack you over the head." He laughed. "But let's get serious, Niccolò! Don't say a word about this to anyone, you understand? I'll help you as much as I can, but don't ask for too much. I'm not safe either." Then he revealed everything to me. "Listen, it seems he's after you, no joke. People say that you messed with his daughter, at least that's what Pere said, the one who saw you sneaking into her house. He got suspended the other day for disobedience, so now he's spreading rumors. At least until Nižetić gets to him, and then . . . ."

He said much more, but the whirl of thoughts in my mind kept me from either hearing or responding. I muttered a couple of incoherent questions, trying to collect my thoughts. From the moment I had regained my senses, the others and I had tried to prepare a defense and kept hoping that we would get a chance to dismiss all the suspicions about us in court. I'd never allowed myself to take Nižetić's threats seriously, the words he'd said only minutes before. In my blindness, I had removed her from everything that was happening to us, convinced that our love was secret, and that it was only waiting for all the misunderstandings to be sorted out in order to be able to continue its anonymous course.

But now it was clear. I understood Nižetić's desire for revenge. I asked Ivan to repeat what he'd told me. I put my head into my hands. When facing disaster, we all become like sheep that stand petrified before the fire and sometimes leap into it. The thought of my father and those who were thrown in prison with him terrified me.

Ivan told me what had been happening since my departure, the public meetings all around the island, the arrests of some groups of Cominform supporters and their transfer to nearby islands under the Velebit, the quick trials and harshness that were here to stay. He also told me about himself, about serving in the police for the last two months. "Why now, goddamn it?" he said dejectedly.

Returning to my case, he asked, "Is what Pere says true, that Nižetić is after you just because of his daughter? I mean, because of you?"

I quickly, in a few minutes, revealed everything from the beginning. Then he told me, with a glance around, what I had not dared to ask. "Almost no one has seen her since then. Nižetić keeps quiet. There are rumors around town that he keeps her tied up inside the house. The other day a woman saw her standing at the window practically naked, shouting something in Italian. People say he grabbed her and pulled her inside. They say they're crazy, the both of them. But . . ." He suddenly stopped and became a guard again. "Attention, Captain!"

Nižetić dismissed him and sat at the other end of the narrow table. All he intended to do with me did not take longer than half a minute. He got up slowly, pulled out his wide police strap without saying anything, put the gun on the table, wrapped one end of the strap around his right hand, stood still for a moment looking straight into my eyes, and then begun hitting me all over with its buckle. He screamed as if in tears, "So you screw other people's daughters ... eh? Eh? Treacherous vermin! Screw my daughter, will you ...."

After a couple of blows I remembered nothing. I lay on the floor while Nižetić struck me all over, especially my stomach and groin, who knows for how long. Ivan told me later that for a couple of minutes the monastery echoed as if someone were being slain in there. I don't know. He destroyed my kidneys and mutilated my body.

The friar came closer to me. He lifted his habit around his abdomen and showed several deep, long scars. I muttered what came to my mind, something just for something's sake, to remove the scene from my eyes. "Horrible."

"Yes. If only that had been all," he said bitterly, "You don't know, child, what horrible is. Surely not how horrible this was. Nobody can know what this was like." He stopped. He seemed insulted by my interference, the inadequacy of my words, their redundancy. He said nothing for a few seconds, and I thought he was finished. But then he sighed, like a swimmer before the final leg of a race, as if gathering his strength.

"Right. Ivan and another guard took me to the cell in that state. They told me later that my father wept like a child and only caressed my hair, lacking the strength to do anything more, while the others tried to help me as well as they knew. I will never forget those people. They nursed me and watched over me and my father's last hours, which began the very next morning and lasted through one day and the night after. He couldn't swallow the water Ivan brought us in secret. His soul departed his body before the dawn of the next morning. All shrunk and tiny, he ended clenching my hand. I heard no last words from him, not a sound even. He died silently. Perhaps because suffering needs no comment."

Chapter the Eighth

Had we been standing next to Maria, who, with her ear pressed against the door to Catarina's chamber, had hardly managed to make out anything of the conversation with Enzo, at the moment when they grew silent, after which only rustling could be heard from inside—of fabric or whispers it was impossible to say—, we would have seen her tears silently dropping onto her thighs. Had we been able to stand next to her for some ten minutes, we would have realized what was going on inside, and, like Maria, we would have risen and left for our quarters. But our hearts would have remained beating quietly in our chests; our minds would not have plotted what Maria's mind then plotted; we would not have been bent on revenge, or, like Maria, already considering the manner of its execution.

Enzo stole out of the room soon after the trumpets had sounded the master's return. It was near three in the morning. Before he left her bed, Catarina explained all the major aspects of the customs she had adopted, the customs that would, she made clear, protect their love, their happiness, beneath the flying Mardi standard. He could not cease to admire the woman's worth. After they'd dressed and set out, he for his room, she for her marital bed, he kissed her several times in the corridor, to which she responded by pressing her finger to his lips in token of caution.

That night he fell into a deep, sound, and silent sleep, the likes of which he had not enjoyed for months. He awoke near the midday meal, perfectly relaxed and happy. He cast a hasty glance at his manuscripts, and just as he was preparing to take up his work in earnest, with renewed energy in body and soul, the bell called him to descend that very moment to the dining hall.

He found the Mardis already seated. Maria, as a close friend, ate in the same room, but, appropriately, at a different table.

"Ah, here is our Enzo, looking very spirited today," remarked old Mardi, offering Enzo a chair beside him.

From excitement and insane happiness, Enzo did not even glance at Catarina, while she, aware of the danger, greeted him almost inaudibly. Maria leaned over her meal and said not a word. Her silence lasted the whole morning, and Catarina was frightened (Perhaps she sensed something? Perhaps she knew?) by such behavior. She decided to talk to her, to find out the cause of her apathy, and also to soothe her own turbulent thoughts.

After the meal, as usual, Mardi began talking about what was happening abroad—the current political situation of his region, his meeting of the night before with the bishop, his new triumphs. In short, those present learned that a group of spies had been caught the morning before at San Benedetto and that each of them had had a piece of black cloth with the iron Hapsburg coat of arms on it, serving them as a sign of recognition and a pass for the border posts. Later he showed them some pieces of the cloth that were, as he pointed out, a part of the war booty, and then continued by telling them that some of the spies were later interrogated by the bishop and his investigator, Fra Giovanni, and that the information which was extracted from them confirmed that the bishop's action was altogether appropriate, but that it was also just the beginning and such actions would need to be continued with greater intensity and support. And that everything should be done in order to avoid the unfortunate destiny of Enzo's homeland.

Mardi added that, after news of the arrest had spread through the county, a multitude had gathered before the bishop's palace, demanding a swift public execution. The execution had been performed the night before by torchlight. Mardi mentioned that this had seemed to pacify the anxious crowd, adding that tax collection for the war was not going well in that some village leaders were protesting against the bishop's measure.

A brief discussion followed in which Enzo was especially active, while Catarina made only occasional remarks and Maria remained disturbingly quiet. He asked Mardi for details of the case, commented on possible political implications, praised the efficiency of the bishop and Mardi's soldiers. The old man seemed especially pleased by the course of the discussion, and, with the wisdom that came from many years' engagement in politics and a generosity that told him not to keep that wisdom to himself but pass it on, he continued speaking at great length so that they left the dining room only some hours later.

Catarina, it must be said, invited the maid to her chambers in order to keep her company as usual, but the latter responded somewhat reticently, saying that she had a terrible headache and that it was already late. These words troubled Catarina a great deal, first, because they seemed unpleasantly familiar, and second, because they were not at all true: it was only three o'clock in the afternoon.

9

They took us from the cell to an improvised courtroom that morning, several hours after his death. I remember flies buzzing around us, as if some of it had been left on our hands and clothes. Three people sat at several tables joined together in the middle of the room, which the Benedictine priests had perhaps used for their meals. These were the judge, the prosecutor, and Petar Nižetić. Several old men and police clerks, representing a jury, were on their right. They sat us on a bench on the left side of the room, beside the state lawyers who'd been assigned to the case.

Believe me, we hadn't even sat down before the judge had opened the case book and called the witnesses. Some were prisoners in gray rags, people I'd never seen before let alone met. They spoke very convincingly about our guilt, accusing my father of organizing an uprising. They did not pass silently over their own guilt, but asked the court to be merciful. The time allotted for our response was short. We denied what was stated and swore we were innocent. Our lawyers only repeated what we had said and asked for milder punishments, even before our guilt had been proven. The jury did not deliberate long. The judge expressed his regret that the main culprit had escaped punishment by his own death, adding that we were as responsible as he. Praising Nižetić's action, he sentenced us to death by firing squad. And that was all the people's authorities had to say about it.

All this flashed before my eyes. I staggered out of the room, and the only thing I remember was the terrified expression on Ivan's face. When they brought us into the cell, we sat silently, apart from one another, as if unaware of the presence of others, as if defending our right to solitude, now as we awaited our final moments. I leaned against the wall, sobbing silently. So this was where it ended. My father was dead. I was living my final days.

Several hours passed in silence. Then somebody moved, asked a question. One Italian seemed as if he'd been waiting for just that in order to begin telling his story. All heads turned in his direction. Everyone listened carefully, without questions or interruptions.

The room had been dark for some time when a guard opened the door and let Ivan in. "Stand up!" he ordered. "The captain has accepted your request to see your father once more."

I did not want to contradict him. I could discern no signal of comfort in his face, so I feared my final hour had come. I said nothing and followed him, unconscious, as I barely lifted my feet, that I was escaping death, on whose list of unfinished tasks were the men I left behind. One of them patted me on the shoulder, which I understood as a final goodbye.

I shivered as we went down that same staircase toward the basement. Ivan's appearance frightened me and I thought how, in the end, we were each alone in our misfortunes. I took his behavior hard, the way one takes the betrayal of those considered friends and benefactors. I reproached him in those minutes, utterly unaware of his noble sacrifice.

Things became clearer to me when he brought me into a dark basement room in the middle of which lay my father. The nearly unbearable stench of a decaying body filled the room, but I knelt before it all the same, took his cold hand into mine and brought it to my face.

Ivan interrupted me: "Hurry if you want to see tomorrow."

Baffled and confused, I watched him unbutton the top of his uniform, lift his collar, remove his handcuffs, and tousle his hair.

"He's dead, and so will you be if you don't step away from him."

He tossed me the keys and directed me to use the middle one to open the padlock on the wooden boards that covered the window from the inside. He said I'd need the smallest for the handcuffs, and I realized what he was doing, understood the insane boy was saving my life. I tried to express my thanks somehow.

"Just be quiet. Listen to me and don't screw up," he warned. "You know it takes less than ten minutes to get from here to the pine grove outside town. That's how long it'll take them to find me and start after you. In the bay in front of the grove, there's a boat. Run toward Italy or somewhere else. You'll have enough time to row a good distance while they're looking for you in town. Now open these shades."

I spread the wooden boards. A window appeared behind them. It was completely dark, without moonlight at all: excellent conditions for saving one's life. He told me to tie him up against the door. Then he ordered me to hit him several times. What could I do? I did what he asked. In the end, in thanks and repentance, I kissed him on the cheek.

"It's clear that that's all you know," were the last words I heard from that extraordinary youth, before he slumped down, pretending to be unconscious.

Chapter the Ninth

Several days passed, whose length, for those in love and those whose blood had been poisoned by vengeance, could not be measured by any instrument known to that age. While Mardi wrote missives, read replies, checked the conditions of his guards here and there, and dedicated more and more time and energy to the village leaders' despotism, which caused the aforementioned intensive correspondence, Catarina's heart was troubled by Maria's ever more frequent absences, her isolation, and obvious ill-humor. But her worries would be whisked away, as if by an implacable wind, by the thought of an invitation from the bishop, a diversion by spies, or any sign of trouble.

During those days Enzo occupied himself with long walks in the surrounding countryside, but his impatience and confusion prevented him from continuing work on his manuscript. This, among other things, is the reason why he never finished his well-known book of poetry. These walks encouraged the thought of possible encounters with her. Catarina, as a sensible and cautious being after all, did not give herself up to these persistent temptations. She wanted least of all to be given away by trifles. Their official communications were limited to the ordinary exchange of basic information, which was after all, required by courtesy. "Courtesy, precisely that," thought Catarina, "That is the way to avoid any suspicion, prevent anyone from ever suspecting that my panties are splitting when I lay eyes on this fellow."

That she had gone too far in her pretended indifference became clear when Mardi scolded her, in a casual conversation, and asked her to treat the young man with more delicacy. She laughed to herself at his advice, but suddenly, as if she had choked on a piece of food, the gloomy thought that the path she was taking offered everything except safety stopped her short.

Nevertheless, on several occasions Enzo squeezed her hand, caressed her knee with the toe of his shoe during the mid-day meal, touched her lips on one of their walks together, and, during one encounter in the stable, when Umberto's brief absence gave them a few moments together, managed to unfasten two of her buttons, though it was, unfortunately, not enough to slip his hand inside her dress. These were their days. This was how their passion was stirred, nourished by frustration and fear. But this was not to last long. That it would have been better if it had, you will agree at the end of my story.

The long awaited day for renewing amorous pleasures had arrived, some thought. Catarina made clear the fact that everything was ready, that her blood was boiling, that, in short, she had lost her head, when she broke into tears and pretended anger upon Mardi's receipt of the bishop's urgent missive, which was brought to him by a panting youth. The old cuckold tried to calm her, citing reasons she had heard at least a hundred times. He bribed her with promises of new hunting expeditions and balls, even offered to build a new villa near the sea. Enzo consoled him on his way out, bidding him good fortune, because duty was duty and women were women. And this woman's abilities, he thought excitedly, watching her tears, seemed inexhaustible.

You needn't believe me, but if even half a minute passed after the tramp of Mardi's personal guard had grown quiet before Catarina felt the uneven surface of the floor on her back for the first time, let lightning split me in two. And who then would have had the time to remember "what will protect our love, dear Enzo"? Who would have had the time to remember that the flag on the main tower had not been raised, that the order to raise it according to the custom created by the mistress had not been issued, that most of the guards did not know of the master's departure and that no trumpet would sound, unless he himself were so wise, or so foolish, as to send a messenger before him, as every good custom requires? Who would have remembered all that under such circumstances, I ask you? Not I, certainly.

Well, so now you see exactly what it was that vengeance was waiting for.

Maria did not need to be told twice that the iron was hot, when Catarina, without saying a word, indeed, as I said, without issuing any order at all, hurried toward her private chambers. This time it seems there's no headache, thought the girl, realizing in a flash that her revenge was now at hand. Oh, the deceived child had already planned everything. And she slowly began to enjoy the feeling, the reversal of roles, the ignorance on their side, the destinies she now tossed in her hands like fragile balls, like, God forgive me, a man's testicles. She paused by the slightly opened window and looked in the direction of the main tower. There was no sign of an incited lynx, no sign of Mardi's banner of loyalty and devotion. With the composure of a croupier who collects other people's bets on a pile and knows that the hand and the money are already lost but who merely smiles courteously while others grow excited and sweaty, with exactly such composure Maria went from the window to her chamber to write, this time a much more effective missive.

Francesco Mardi knew immediately that something was wrong when he saw the frightened Umberto at the door of the bishop's palace. The bishop's ill temper alone, at the interruption of his meeting, was enough to make Mardi's face darken with every step he took toward the palace exit. On one hand, there was the bishop and the expression of disdain on the faces of the assembled noblemen when the batman had explained to them that the honorable Master Mardi had been called from this important gathering by none other than his stable boy. On the other was a growing concern that had already begun to prick his heart, because, damn it, something must have happened.

"Why have you interrupted me in my work, Umberto?" said Mardi sternly as he appeared at the entrance.

"Master," Umberto said quickly, rushing forward. "I didn't even finish unsaddling the horses when a woman with a veiled face came in—who knows who she was—and told me not to dawdle but deliver this message to you. It had to do with traitors and spies, she said, and I remembered, Master, your speech and your orders and hurried to bring you the letter, because it may be very important."

Realizing that the boy was only talking about some letter, Mardi felt relieved. He waved away all the horrible, dark visions that had arisen before his eyes, grew angry and reprimanded Umberto: What he had done was unacceptable except under the most urgent of circumstances, certainly in the case of some woman in disguise. If this turned out to be some trifle, then by God, he would forfeit a month's salary. These words left a visible mark on Umberto's face. He tried to say something about his loyalty but stopped when the master began unfolding the letter. He understood quickly that his cries were not helping, and a glimmer of hope that this letter might indeed be most urgent, that the message it contained might be extremely important, wiped the previous expression from his face.

Mardi opened the letter, moved it to approximately half a meter away from his eyes and, before he began reading, gave Umberto a look which spoke for itself: "We understand each other then!"

Boiling water could not have burned so much. Nor could the effect of the words Mardi read be described by naming all the ingredients of an old woman's worst poisons, the likes of which simmer in the soul and simultaneously freeze the heart. The pain of the moments during which he read the message, several times bringing the paper close to his face and then moving it away again, could only be described by those unfortunates who have been executed by a faulty guillotine: once and for all. Then again.

When there were no more reasons to doubt, Mardi had only to shout, "To your horses, brothers!" and his guards began to appear from around the corners of the building. But as the young men saw that their master was already hurrying for home, they too hurriedly mounted their horses. Umberto followed them slowly, and he seemed to be feeling a bulge of silver coins in his left pocket. In the seconds that passed after Mardi had screamed his command and leaped to his horse, the paper that had caused such panic floated to the ground. Had someone accidentally picked it up (someone who could read), he would have read the following stylized words:

While you chase spies in the woods,
One sleeps
At your wife's bosom

A friend

While Mardi raced to save his home and honor, trying to fathom all the possible significance of the strange message and discover its friendly author, in the quiet of the castle two young hearts enjoyed the sweet fruit of their — they still believed — secret love. And who could have convinced them otherwise at that moment? Who could have made them, say, open the window and glance through it to the main tower, remind the guards to stay alert and, by God, not fail to announce the master's return, et cetera, in short, to preserve their love and, more importantly, their lives? For as he approached his home, it became more and more clear to Mardi that someone's blood would spill.

Mardi pulled his horse up short on a hill before the castle. A single glance made him painfully accept the accuracy of the message Umberto had delivered: no flag flew atop the main tower. He could see only two guards on the castle walls. This was enough to convince him that tonight he would hear no trumpets and that that, dammit, was perhaps the only good thing about it.

To protect himself from the possible eagerness of some of his men, Mardi sent a messenger forward with the sole command that they should not sound their instruments in the usual manner upon seeing his suite before the gate. He ordered complete silence. The glance he cast at her windows, the light he saw coming from those chambers in the midst of the night, made his old heart forget all possible explanations, dismiss all excuses.

They entered the castle, as ordered, without a sound. Mardi stopped his men before the entrance. He wanted to go alone, but a hint of possible danger made him take along two guards. Inside, everything was silent and deserted, just as Mardi thought, and he climbed the stairs slowly and with difficulty. He passed the first floor. Maria stood behind the door to her quarters, listening as his step advanced toward the love nest, where it would wring those birds' necks, and she would know her revenge. It is hard to say what she must have felt at that moment of realization — relish or rage, pride or sorrow, rapture or despair?

When he had climbed to the third floor and reached the master chambers, glanced at his predecessors, at the proud foreheads and firm hands that had earned all that surrounded him here, he recalled the feeling of honor he had enjoyed since childhood, while the restrained grins that hung above his crouched slink, suggesting that his otherwise proud pedigree had gone astray, made him feel like a stranger, a spy, a thief in his own house, and he took it hard. And so, exhaling completely, as if ridding himself of mercy with the expelled air, he said to himself, "Let us deal with this matter honorably, Francesco."

Because not so long ago we stood beside Maria, it is needless to say what Mardi heard when he put his ear to the door: commotion, giggling, a loud sigh now and then, a clinking of glasses, and, most importantly, the snake's name. Oh, nothing is as painful as a betrayal of one's generosity. Everything blurred before his eyes. He felt a pounding in his chest. He tried to shake free of some unpleasant thought, which made him stumble against the objects around him. He did not feel his legs. All he felt, while two guards kept him from collapsing, was the desire, before he dropped dead, to see her beautiful head on the block. That scene gave him strength to root out childish thoughts. He opened the door abruptly and took a firm step toward the face of truth.

Had she ever looked more beautiful? Hard to say, seeing her satisfied in another man's arms. But this lasted only a moment. Then the beautiful face was scarred with horror, as if by a quick sword thrust. Enzo jumped aside and, before he could try to reach the window, he heard the strident command: "Seize the spy!"

10

Soon I reached the monastery garden. Completely taken up as I was with Ivan's orders, I hadn't even glanced at my father, and for a moment I wanted to go back to the basement cell to see him. But the loud voices of the guards shouting at the entrance to the monastery, now on my right, made me rush toward the pine grove. I tell you this because my soul was pressed upon by the fact that I was leaving him without a proper goodbye. It's hard to say exactly, but perhaps that was the reason I did what I did, turning back toward my own house, not toward the salvation of the grove.

I avoided the main streets, choosing foot paths, crossing gardens, and taking byways, and very quickly reached our house. The garden and the house lay in complete darkness. Ivanka was not there, so I felt brave enough to see my mad decision through to the end and satisfy the pitiful desire of providing proof of loyalty to my dead father, for I imagine that was my reason: to do something we're never prepared for while we believe there's still time before us.

I took a shovel from the tool shed, and — I can see you know where I went.

"Under the fig tree," I said.

The friar nodded, content. "Under the fig tree," he repeated and continued his tale.

Two feet down I found the barrel from my father's story. At that moment I heard sounds and voices making their way through the dark, quiet night from the monastery. The manhunt had begun. I opened the barrel quickly, breaking into it with a shovel. Inside was a small piece of silk-like fabric which I opened. At first, in the darkness, I could not make anything out. I raised it above my head, turning it in my hands, looking for a trace of light. Then I caught sight of the flag's reddish glitter. I went toward the house and in a moment managed to climb onto the roof, according to my father's wish, which now came sadly true — in confirmation of what Petra did not want to know, and proof that even defeat has its own banner.

The pursuit had spread quickly. The whole town had been alerted by the time I realized it was the moment to save myself. I heard footsteps and voices around nearly every corner. I had to sneak carefully through the streets, watch for people coming out of their homes, run into passages and hide when I heard a vehicle or a police patrol approaching. Nevertheless, after a bit more than half an hour I came down to the pine grove and found the boat. Once again I commended Ivan's soul to God and began to row, fearing all the while that someone might see me from the shore or intercept me in the open sea. I realized that Ivan had planned my escape only to this point and that from now on the darkness and my own strength were my only chance of reaching Italian waters before dawn.

And that's what happened. I rowed through the chamber of that God given darkness. I rowed frantically through the black, into the night. I know today that life awaited me at one end, while at the other was memory. I realize now that it's possible to live one's life by embalming the past. Between you and me, people of such ungrateful ilk are everywhere you look.

Chapter the Tenth

She covered her head with a pillow and sobbed loudly without even trying to cover her nakedness. They dragged Enzo, absolutely speechless, bare-bottomed and pale with fear, toward the basement, through the corridors that had begun filling with soldiers and subjects awakened by the bells.

Catarina merely shuddered when the door slammed. Mardi stood there motionless and firm.

"If you want to keep your life," he began quietly, like a man resigned to his bitter fate, "you will do so only as my wife. This house will see no scandal. Soon we will search through his chambers, after which everyone will know that yet another spy has been discovered in the region and that Francesco Mardi himself has prevented the violation of his own wife. You will tell the bishop's investigators what really happened; that is, you will confirm before the bishop's chief investigator, Fra Giovanni, what I will announce to the bishop and the people tomorrow morning."

He gave special emphasis to his final words, then paused briefly in order to make himself still clearer and more credible, and finally continued, raising his voice slightly: "Now then. You'll say that you caught him going through my things two hours after I rode from the castle, that he attacked you and dragged you into your room, bound you, and tried to force himself upon you, but he could not go through with it because I saved you at the last moment. That is, my dear, you were saved by a message that I received from the castle, delivered to me by Umberto, in which a good soul informed me that Enzo was sneaking through my chambers, performing his devious duties, which were the reason he came here from the north." Then, as if speaking to himself, he added, "Enzo, that snake in the heart."

Mardi was quiet for some moments, and then, before leaving the room, he said: "I hope I've made myself clear?" He waited for another moment, but there was no answer. "All right," he concluded. "I'm glad to see we agree on something at least."

Mardi sent Maria and several other girls to Catarina's room where they found her pulling her hair out, screaming and striking her body with her fists. They struggled with her until the morning, when, under the influence of countless tranquilizers, she at last fell asleep. It could be said that, witnessing Catarina's madness, Maria felt repentant for the first time. In the days that followed, Enzo's quick downfall, Catarina's advanced illness, her empty glances and muteness, together with the questions of the bishop's investigator, Fra Giovanni, which lasted for hours on end, transformed that remorse into inevitable despair. Despite everything, it must be admitted, she remained true to herself in her revenge.

*

Having left Catarina's chambers, Mardi knew that the defense of his honor was only half complete. The betrayal, deception, falsehood, and deaths to follow made him rest for several minutes. But he quickly snapped out of his numbness and, just as he began writing the first letter to his captain of the guards, reflected that life was a turncoat and a whore. Nor did this idea abandon him as he was completing the second letter, in which he informed the bishop of the discovery that had forced him to leave the meeting, of the latest success in the bishop's mission, and the urgency of action. In short, the bishop was told that Mardi had discovered a spy in his own house, but that this was not the end of the matter, for he was convinced that some of the guards and village leaders were involved with the enemy. "This obviously explains," he wrote in conclusion, "their lack of cooperation."

His writing complete, Mardi scattered his papers across the room, turned drawers inside out, and upended several chairs. He then went into Enzo's room, ordering his lieutenant and secretary to accompany him.

We may note that the consequence of the first letter was the arrest of the two guards who, together with Mardi, had apprehended his wife and Enzo together, shall we say, *in flagranti*. Indeed, just after they had removed their heavy boots sometime before early morning, and dozed off on their pallets, they were awakened by heavy blows between which they barely managed to grasp the absolutely incomprehensible accusation of collaboration with the enemy. The outcome of the second letter would be seen on the following morning, when the bishop's guards, led by Fra Giovanni, reached the castle gate.

*

What was put into the logbook that night?

I note here the possessions enumerated by Master Francesco Mardi and his lieutenant, Giuliano Sesso, who examined the quarters of the accused Enzo Strecci.

A desk containing pens (three items), an inkstand (half empty), sheets of paper filled out from top to bottom in regular lines, though of uneven length (seventy items). Contents irrelevant.

A chest of drawers beside the bed containing apple seeds (four items), an empty glass smelling of brandy (one item), a leather bound book on whose cover is written *Il Canzoniere*, "The Singer" (one item, numerous pages).

A closet containing tight fitting chintz trousers (two items), silk underwear (ten items), a gold-trimmed plush undergarment (one item), white flaxen shirts (seven items), three chintz jackets (white, yellow, azure), among which a concealed piece of small black fabric was discovered, with an iron coat of arms on which a two-headed eagle with legs apart could be recognized; one half-empty half-liter bottle (of brandy).

This concludes the logbook upon Master Mardi's request, for sufficient evidence against the accused Enzo Strecci has been discovered.

Signed,

Francesco Mardi, Master
Giuliano Sesso, Lieutenant
Fulvio Bosso, Scribe

And what was placed into the logbook of Fra Giovanni, the bishop's investigator?

The Statement of Mardi:

Thank God, someone caught sight of the beast I had taken into my house like my own son, as he sallied through my chambers. You ask me why that worthy message, which I lost somewhere in the commotion, was anonymous? I suppose the good soul was frightened by the degree of kindness my wife and I had so openly bestowed upon the gentleman such that, it could be said, he became a minor deity in the house. So I left the meeting suddenly, realizing what was going on, understanding that I'd been betrayed in such a vile way. Two guards came with me. The way Enzo addressed them while they dragged him down the corridor, saying all the time, "Don't, brothers!" and crying, "Don't you recognize me? It's me, Enzo!" That and my long political experience in dealing with such people made me suspicious. That morning they were taken to be interrogated, while Lieutenant Sesso and I found among their belongings something that confirmed my presentiment — two cockades on a dark cloth.

They claim there was no attempted rape at all, according to what they saw, is that it? Ha. Well, does that require comment? Never mind, quite all right. I know you're just doing your duty. Indeed, you have performed it well to this day at least, Fra Giovanni. You are sure you do not need anything else? Still, I will add something. The servants can confirm that, a day after we arrested those spies at San Benedetto, Strecci asked me questions about the action for hours after our meal. My kindness, dear Giovanni, blinded me.

The Statement of Maria:

Don't ask me anything about politics; I don't know anything. I couldn't even suspect something like this would happen. When he had just arrived, he stood in the corridor before the master's door like a pigeon in the rain. Had I known what I know now, I would have understood from his glare, which was focused at Mistress Catarina, that he was up to something. I can tell you what I know, and what everybody knows, and that is that he displayed his perverse passion during the hunt and on numerous occasions during lunch, and that he would dance around her the minute the master left the castle. It's not her fault, it's his. Excuse me? You're asking if it's true that I was in love with him? What? I told everyone he'd be my fiancé? I shall say only two words about that—verily, let me fall into the abyss if I lie: No. Never.

The Statement of Umberto:

I never liked that Lombardian pretty boy. I knew
he was up to something from the beginning, when
he took that lute out of my hands and exclaimed:
"It will be just like Milan here!" Who was he
speaking to, I ask you? I saw him, strolling and
strutting, especially during the last couple of days,
and then he went straight into my stable, asked
how many horses I had, which was the fastest, then
this then that. The fellow asked questions. I was
suspicious. And just look where he ended up. Yes
sir, I saw through him from the start.

The Statement of Little Bepo:

That is some strange man. He hit me twice so hard
that it still hurts when I touch the spot. Just like
that. A violent man. No wonder he got caught up
in such business. His kind hits whether he gets
what he wants or not. He never asks the same
question twice. That's my opinion. I remember
one of his questions very clearly: He asked a lot
about whether the master often left the castle. And
when I met him walking in the fields, he would
give me a strange look. Now it's clear to me, he'd
prop himself up and tip his head a bit to the side.
They call such people dreamers. And then we'd

have a long talk. He was interested in everything,
my mother, the old man ... Sorry? Is that all, you
say? So have I helped at all?

The Statement of Niccolò Brizzi, Village Leaders'
Representative:

I swear on Mary, Mother of God that I never saw
the man, neither I nor any of the village leaders,
and that he is not, as you claim, our chief. We love
our homeland and Master Mardi, and we would
never. . . What? Why didn't we pay the required
quarter? Well, I already talked about that with the
bishop, and he promised me he would consider the
matter. Look, I'm telling you for the hundredth
time, people are starving. Draft everyone you like,
but don't take the bread from their plates. Excuse
me, what Habsburg ornaments were found among
our belongings?! What are you talking about? In
my house?!

The Statement of Catarina:

Two hours after the master rode from the castle, I
caught Enzo going through his things. He attacked
me and dragged me into my room, bound me, and
attempted to force himself on me but was stopped
when my husband came to my rescue at the last
moment; that is, I was saved by the message that
was sent from the castle, the one Umberto brought
to Rimini, in which a happy little soul declared

that Enzo had been seen rummaging through the master's chamber and performing his espionage duties because of which he came from the north, Enzo, that sweet snake in the heart....

There follows Fra Giovanni's commentary:

In concurrence with Francesco Mardi, much to my relief, I here cease the questioning of the victim, whose physical appearance and incoherent, unclear testimony has left no doubt that her state—after the Habsburg spy, Enzo Strecci, attempted to violate her according to the accumulated evidence—is that of advanced madness. Let God grant peace to her soul.

The Final Chapter

Let it be remembered that the rain fell heavily upon the heads of those citizens gathered at Rimini's Trinity Square. Despite the rain, they awaited the execution patiently. Enzo came before the crowd, trembling like some frail animal. He was a bit surprised, though only for a moment, when he saw two well beaten youths and after them three village leaders who, blue with bruises after a ten-day torture, were thrown before his feet and told to admit that, to ease their souls before the world and God, Enzo Strecci was a rebel commander. As I said, his surprise lasted only a moment, for he knew the logic of power better than any risqué lines he might have penned. The youths confessed, the whip cracking audibly over their backs, and their heads were cut off first. Next the other three were decapitated without their saying a word. It must be said that with his head on the block Enzo Strecci could not see the sea a mere twenty paces away. Instead he saw an utter grayness that reached from the water to the sky. And then it was as if a black standard covered his eyes.

11

The friar stopped talking, and I thought his story had ended. I
wanted to say something, but he was quicker:
"So you won't ask what happened to her?"
"I wanted to."
"I'd tell you anyway, because everything I told you this
afternoon and evening would be incomplete without Petra's
end. And, of course, her father's too."

Several years after my escape, I met a man from my homeland
in Rome. He said he had arrived in Italy a year after me, and
I hurriedly asked about her fate. What he told me made me
think that the circle of suffering would never end, that I was its
center, he whom death enclosed but who remained safe from
it, he who was forced by fate to repent for his own guilt and
regret, but never die.

The morning after I left, she was dead. She had leaped from
the tower of Saint Mary's, the tallest and loveliest bell tower on
Rab, landing at the feet of her father and the crowd. The man

said that she had laughed hysterically as she climbed to its top, pointing in the direction of our house, where a red flag flew. Then she had jumped. He told me that Nižetić had lost control completely when they took him away. She was buried in the Rab cemetery as a suicide, quiet and lonely.

No one ordered the flag to be taken down. It flew above my father's house until the wind tore it apart. This happened before Nižetić had recovered and been transferred to the nearby prison island, where, due to the nature of the times, he soon lost his position as warden of that unfortunate institution, and ended up being trampled by his former prisoners.

When the friar spoke the last sentences of his story and dropped his eyes to his lap, as if wearily lowering a curtain on a stage where too many difficult scenes had been played, only then did I become aware that Castello Mardi had fallen into the deep dark of night. But it was nothing like the night of the friar's escape. For I could see the moon and the sky brimming with stars as I stood and approached the window.

The story was all told. Several minutes went by without either of us saying a word. I wanted to continue the conversation somehow, but the friar did not raise his eyes. At that moment the sound of the car horn could be heard from the other side of the yard, another world, it seemed to me, and, for the first time in hours, I remembered the two girls with whom I'd discovered this man, whose story had made me see incredible things and whom now I had to leave.

It was as if he'd been waiting for just this. He stood up and said mockingly, "That would be your friends, Bosnian, whom you abandoned for the unpleasant friar. It seems it's finally time to leave his presence."

"I had almost forgotten about them," I said in all honesty.

He placed his hand on my shoulder and concluded our short-lived association with the words, "That's not good, in truth. What will they say now? Come on then. Better go. I'll see you to the exit. I've kept you too long as it is with my stories."